the IMPERFECT COMPROMISE

HILLARY AND TRUMP:

ONE YEAR TO SHARE THE PRESIDENCY AND REMAKE THE ELECTION SYSTEM

A VOTER'S GUIDE BY

HARRIS GRAY

THE IMPERFECT COMPROMISE
PUBLISHED BY Harris Gray
Copyright © 2016 by Harris Gray
ISBN 978-0988895782

This is a work of fiction. Names, characters, places and incidents are either the product of the author's imagination or are used fictitiously, and any resemblance to actual per-sons, living or dead, business establishments, events or locales is entirely coincidental.

Printed in the USA.

IMAGES OF DONALD TRUMP AND HILLARY CLINTON VIA WIKIPEDIA COMMONS
https://commons.wikimedia.org/wiki/File:Hillary_Clinton_official_Secretary_of_State_portrait_crop.jpg

https://commons.wikimedia.org/wiki/File:Donald_Trump_August_19_2015.jpg

FORWARD

S O HERE WE ARE, STUCK in the middle of the craziest presidential
campaign in history. The United States is 1 month away from a potentially world-shaking election. We're faced with a choice that is arguably
odious, but certainly monumental.

How to decide? Pundits have analyzed our candidates' characters and
plumbed their pasts, all to tell you who Hillary Clinton and Donald
Trump *are*. But what would they *do*? Perhaps like you, we just couldn't
imagine what a Trump or Hillary presidency would look like. So we
decided to do exactly that; we imagined it.

Actually we thought it would be easy to picture a Hillary presidency.
The main themes: Governing through gridlock. (We assume Democrats
take the Senate and Republicans maintain control of the House.) A push
to cement the Obama gains and advance Hillary's pet causes. And Congressional investigations all the while.

But there is much to be discovered during an event-rich thought
experiment; and our "2017: Year of the Imperfect Compromise" includes
a murderer's row of foreign and domestic crises. We're political junkies
who have enjoyed decades of media and insider accounts of our government, much of it starring Hillary and her extended circle of intimates. So
we felt comfortable role-playing Hillary's actions in our what-if world,
and intrigued by what unfolded.

And then there's Trump. Sure he's made a lot of promises (and threats)
about what a Trump presidency looks like. But he's never operated in
government. It's safe to assume things won't go and people won't play
the way he'd like. We have a candidate who prides himself on unpredict-
ability, who has no idea what's coming. That made our job fun and the
results surprising.

A word about the twists & turns necessary to arrive at a 1-year split
presidency, the "Imperfect Compromise." Like any good fantasy writer,
we need to create a convincing, "real" alternate reality. The probability of
all the events that cause our election debacle to occur might be low; but
all of them have been ripped from the headlines, as they say. We think

you'll recognize the terrible plausibility. And perhaps you'll agree that our presidential election system needs improvement. Maybe you'll even like our solution....

We conceived this voter's guide on a mid-August whim and finished it minutes before the 1st debate on September 26. It's short and it's sweet and it's undoubtedly as incomplete as the Compromise we describe. We could never delve into all the policy choices our potential presidents will contemplate, or anticipate all the crises they will face. But we hit quite a few!

Now it's time to give our voter's guide a whirl and join us in near-future Washington D.C. for the story of 2 possible presidencies. Come find us at **HarrisGray.com** and let us know what you think. And then as you prepare to cast your vote, remember what that really old Crusader told Harrison Ford as he struggled to identify the Grail: Choose wisely....

COMPLETE CHAOS & IMPERFECT COMPROMISE

THE CLOAK ROOM COMPROMISE OF 1876. The Hanging Chad Supreme Court Decision of 2000. These two presidential elections, 124 years apart, exposed the flaws in our election process. Yet no popular outcry resulted, and no progress or significant change in the system has ever taken place.

The Electoral College is flawed. It's meant to protect citizens in small states from irrelevancy, but it doesn't. In fact it doesn't treat big-state citizens very well either. The electoral vote is generally winner-take-all in each state, and most of our states are solidly Democrat or Republican. Thus the candidates focus nearly all their campaign resources on a handful of states—the "swing" states—that make up only 1/3 of the population.

That's not what our Framers intended. Now here we are in the midst of a clusterfluff of a presidential election. Hillary Clinton won the electoral vote over Donald Trump by a substantial margin, 352 to 186. But it doesn't feel right, it's too lopsided. The popular vote was 45.5% Clinton, 44.5% Trump, 7% Johnson, 3% Stein.

A glaring light shone upon the disparity between the popular and electoral votes. On top of that, and it was something we knew was coming but again seemed powerless or unwilling to prevent, there were so many instances of votes being mishandled, voter intimidation and outright fraud. Hacking occurred in several states. It was too much for the country to bear.

After the November 8th election chaos, the US government had to do something and quickly. Yet the 9th and the 10th came and went. The country was dumbstruck. A storm was brewing. Faced with an oncoming devastating hurricane, the government's emergency actions were like nailing sheets of plywood to the windows of our houses, as if to say, stay inside and don't look out, and soon the trouble will pass; meanwhile waves of frustration and then anger flooded the streets.

The candidates did not help the climate. Hillary defiantly told America in no uncertain terms that she won and the Donald lost. Trump did not ask for demonstrations and riots but he would not denounce them. Trump said he understood the desire and need to demonstrate and riot. In the week that followed the election there were 29 deaths and countless injuries. Cities across the country implemented strict curfews; in a few cities martial law was declared. Texas lawmakers screamed for succession from the Union. The people in Texas and around the country seemed to be okay with it. In the days that followed, the Dow Jones dropped below 10,000 and a worldwide economic crisis began.

LET THE HACKING BEGIN. In Portland, Oregon, the system was hacked and write-in votes for Bernie Sanders seemed to count for Hillary. In Miami-Dade county in Florida, 90% of the vote went to Trump. Almost a week later, almost the entire state of Arizona was still not accounted for and officials didn't know when the votes would be tallied. In Chicago, the old adage, "early and often," was in full swing.

The United State Postal Service had hundreds if not thousands of lost bags. (This after earlier in 2016 discovering 2 bags of ballots from the 2000 presidential election in a back corner of a Florida post office.) There were ballot barcodes that did not match and bar codes that they could not confirm. Everyone was pointing fingers, at hackers. The Democratic National Committee blamed Russia and the Republican National Committee. The RNC blamed China, the DNC and Ukraine. Conspiracy theorists came out of the woodwork. The election debacle gave them a platform and almost none of them sounded crazy anymore.

They sounded legitimate. The X-Files said it best. TRUST NO ONE.

The government scrambled for a solution. Every day that passed, really, every moment that passed without a solution, the government was at risk. It risked more demonstrations, economic collapse, riots and death. Some people feared that the government was crumbling. Others reveled in it.

Of course it made good television.

Hillary was curiously quiet. She asked for peaceful demonstrations and to let the process work as it already had for 220-plus years. But the anger encouraged by Trump and backed by the RNC was resonating with people more than ever. Americans didn't have to agree with Trump or his campaign to decide that the system couldn't continue this way.

We were the laughingstock of the world. Other countries made fun of the "Greatest Nation On Earth." We appeared impotent, and we risked our adversaries taking advantage of our weakness. Trump echoed this loudly, proclaiming the need to revamp the system and hold a reelection ASAP.

By November 13th, together the Supreme Court, Congress and the Obama administration realized they could not fix the problem immediately. Yet immediate action was needed. The mere suggestion that Obama remain in office was offensive to everyone (including President Obama). They decided to convene a special presidential election commission, dubbed SPEC or the Knowledgeable Nine. Or the Nonsense Nine as some would refer to them over the next year. The 9 consisted of the 2 highest-ranking Democrats and Republicans in each chamber of Congress along with the Chief Justice of the Supreme Court:

> *Joe Biden - Outgoing Vice President and President of the Senate (D)*
> *Dick Durbin - Incoming Senate Majority Leader (D)*
> *Mitch McConnell - Senate Minority Leader (R)*
> *John Cornyn - Senate Minority Whip (R)*
> *Paul Ryan - Speaker of the House (R)*
> *Kevin McCarthy - House Majority Leader (R)*
> *Nancy Pelosi - House Minority Leader (D)*
> *Steny Hoyer - House Minority Whip (D)*
> *John Roberts - Chief Justice of the Supreme Court*

The 9 retreated to Camp David. Their mission was to figure out the election and stabilize the country, if not the world.

Each of them agreed that no matter how flawed the system is, under the existing rules Hillary won. Now, how to put her in office? Most just said, *Put her in office, now.* Don't wait for the inauguration, do it now before the US destabilizes further.

Others said, *We wait.* Obama just needs to fully endorse Hillary's victory, the country will stabilize, and Hillary will take office with the inauguration on January 20th. Paul Ryan noted that was exactly what Obama did just hours after the election. The president had said that even though the election did not go off without a hitch, the results needed to be followed. He had given a hearty congratulations to Hillary Clinton and complimented "the other candidates" for their game efforts.

Obama's comments were met with the Dow Jones dropping 6,000 points the following day and subsequent drops since; riots in the street; and death threats to Hillary and other government officials. Anger and resentment were the words of the day.

And it wasn't just the talking heads. The citizens of the US—and not just the radicals—were demanding change. People from all walks of life were wondering what the hell went wrong with their country?

Obama had backed off his stance a bit and asked the country to let the SPEC process play out. It appeared as though Obama couldn't wait to get out of office, taking a hands-off approach to the election crisis. Congress was worried about being voted out of office entirely. Meanwhile the national guard was deployed in several states and police officers were threatening to stay home in fear for their lives.

On the 14th the SPEC-9 made Clinton and Trump meet. The rivals traded barbs, before, during and after the meeting. Neither looked very presidential. Clinton went into hiding less than 12 hours later after 2 attempts on her life. Trump said that trying to kill "that woman" was a real bad idea, that she should be in jail instead.

So, the 9 plodded on. Early on the 15th, more bad news. Word came in about new election fraud. According to the USPS Inspection Service, it looked as if postal fraud had occurred across the country and may take weeks or months to sort out. Fires, vandalism, and demonstrations both peaceful and riotous followed within hours. The 9 were against the wall. The people clamored for drastic measures.

To make matters worse, much, much worse, Thursday, November 17th 2016 happened. All season, a fair number of NFL players had followed Colin Kaepernick's lead by sitting down during the national anthem in protest, demanding social justice for the African American community. Despite the ongoing coverage of black deaths at the hands of the police, the great majority of the public saw the players' protest as a slap in the face to America, Americans and especially the men and women who fought for our country.

Now came word that the Carolina Panthers and New Orleans Saints would kneel in protest during the national anthem before their Thursday night NFL game. Their protest would be for social justice of *all* Americans in the face of the absurd and flawed voting system.

That night as the teams knelt during the anthem, fans in the stands gave them a mix of applause and boos. As the game started, there was a commotion on the sideline. The Panthers' coaches were seen in animated argument with their quarterback, Cam Newton. When the Panthers took the field, Newton knelt on the sideline. The Panthers' backup quarterback ran onto the field as the crowd booed Newton. Some of his teammates congratulated him and others scowled and berated him.

After 3 ineffective plays, the Panthers punted the ball. The crowd became quiet. On the Saints' sideline, quarterback Drew Brees was kneeling. So were quite a few of his teammates. A few players took the field. The Saints' backup quarterback knelt next to Brees. Now there was a chorus of boos with a smattering of cheers.

The Saints' coach called a timeout and the entire team gathered around him. He was super animated, super angry. Drew Brees talked for a few moments, and his teammates knelt in unison. Then the entire Saints team crossed the field to the Panthers side, shook their hands, and walked into the tunnel and to their locker room. The Panthers followed soon after.

A news conference was quickly convened. Sitting at the standard post-game interview table, Drew Brees addressed the reporters and the nation.

"Without my gift, my talent, I would be in the same boat as most Americans. Living paycheck to paycheck. Whether it's flooding here in Louisiana or electing our leaders, we need to be inclusive, not exclusive. We need to help each other out. We need to be heard. This country was founded on a promise, that we are all created equal. Well, it doesn't feel equal when our votes are not counted. That promise has been broken."

He took the hand of Cam Newton seated next to him. Together they stood. Brees raised Newton's hand above their heads. "One man, one vote," said Brees. He said it again and Cam echoed, "One man, one vote." Then the quarterbacks shouted "One man, one vote!" Their teammates joined them on the dais and chanted, "ONE MAN, ONE VOTE! ONE MAN, ONE VOTE!"

Someone whispered in Brees' ear and pretty soon they changed the chant to "ONE PERSON, ONE VOTE!"

It's one thing to have voter fraud, riots and death across America, and the beginning of a worldwide economic collapse. It's another to mess with NFL games. ESPN, bars across America and fantasy football would be destroyed. The media, NFL, Congress and especially the people were going crazy. The 9 needed to fix this before Sunday's NFL games were canceled.

It was November 18th and the 9 had been in constant meetings for 3 days now and felt like they were no closer to a resolution. There was surprisingly little arguing among them. The Republicans outnumbered the Democrats 5-4 but you wouldn't know it by the discussions. They were passionate, not heated, talking as if America was truly on the brink. They were motivated and a bit scared. They worked hard, with few complaints. The meetings were mostly marked with frustration, confusion and disbelief. Not anger but heartbreak; it was just so hard to understand how things had gotten so bad, so quickly.

On November 19th, the 9 emerged from Camp David. They looked haggard and beaten down—but they came out with a decision on how to go forward.

"The election system is broken," said Chief Justice Roberts. "The government will fix it. But it will take time. We need a year to revamp the election process."

In the meantime, the 9 had come up with a compromise. They gave the election to both candidates. Both Hillary Clinton and Donald Trump were given the White House job.

The first 6 months would be Trump's presidency. Then, Clinton would take over for 6 months. The final vote on this compromise was 5 to 4. They would not disclose which way everyone voted, but Roberts assured the country that the vote had not split on partisan lines, and that none of them was happy with the result.

"To stabilize the country," said Roberts, "we had to find compromise. Often the best compromises make no one happy. No one is satisfied. But we are at a turning point in our country. Let's get together. Let's work hard for the next 12 months and then start fresh.

"We will have a solution by October 15th, in time to implement it for 2018 and beyond. The election process will be rebuilt from the ground up. Brick by brick if need be. When it is done, we will have an election process that is fair for all. We will overcome this challenge, as America always does."

Clinton and Trump grudgingly agreed. On inauguration day, January 20th, 2017, Trump would assume the presidency for 6 months. Followed by Clinton for 6 months.

Oddly enough, even though absolutely no one liked the solution, a calmness came over the country. The Imperfect Compromise struck a chord with the American people. Plus, the NFL games would go on.

TRUMP

INTERNATIONAL

REACTION

O N FRIDAY JANUARY 20TH, 2017, President Barack Obama handed over the keys to the White House to Donald J. Trump. President-in-Waiting Hillary R. Clinton and 50 of her closest staffers retired to a newly created office in the East Wing. President Trump took the reins.

"My fellow Americans," Trump addressed the nation that evening. "I am extremely honored to be your president. Very honored. I have a great team ready to hit the ground running. Tonight. A great team, the greatest team this country has ever seen. Since Lincoln and his team of rivals.

"But this team is together. We have one goal: to make America great again.

"Nothing else is important. If America is great, which has not been the case for a long time, a long time. That's when our people are great. You'll have jobs. So many jobs you'll have to choose which job you want.

"And you'll be safe. So safe.

"You're going to remember how good it feels, not to worry about your kids, your grandkids, your wife, your partner. They'll be safe from terrorists and criminals who are in this country illegally. Those people are not happy to see me in this office, let me tell you. Six months from now, maybe they'll just wait until then to try something. God forbid, I hope not. We'll see."

President Trump talked for another 20 minutes. He wrapped it up with this.

"No one talks about the hair anymore. That's a good thing, okay? The comments about the hair, they're fine. I like the hair. Big fan. But we have more important things to focus on, okay? So I'm glad the media has stopped focusing on the hair.

"The next 6 months are going to be amazing. I don't know what will happen after that, to be honest. You won't be able to wait for my next 6 months, I'll tell you that. Assuming they don't get our election system mess figured out. Which I don't think they will, to be honest.

"A lot of presidents have a plan for their first 90 days. I have a 30-day plan. Why wait 3 months? If 3 months is good, 1 month is great. That's what you have to look forward to. A great month and a great half a year.

"Thank you. God bless America."

That night Russian troops moved east out of Russia's Baltic Sea "exclave" of Kaliningrad, into Lithuania, and west from Russia's northwest territories, into Latvia. Some ethnic Russians in these Baltic states welcomed the invasion. They claimed oppression at the hands of the Lithuanian and Latvian government-backed thugs, and the injustice of under-representation, citing the American precedent of the right to self-determination.

"To protect human rights we must take all steps necessary," said Russian president Vladimir Putin at a Kremlin press conference. By 6 a. m. Eastern Standard Time Saturday, Russian troops had for the first time since NATO's creation engaged a member's army.

As President Trump's communications liaison, I was included in his security council meeting Saturday morning. All the expected cabinet and security officials were there, state, defense, NSC, CIA, etc. Before everyone was seated with their coffees, Trump raised his eyebrows and said, "So? What does everyone think?"

Secretary of State Newt Gingrich went first. "The Russian invasion clearly triggers the NATO mutual defense provisions. We'll coordinate with—"

"We put a million troops on the border," said Trump.

"Which border?" said Secretary of Defense David Petraeus.

"The Baltic," said Trump.

"Lithuania," Gingrich clarified. "Northern Poland."

"One million," Trump repeated with extreme enunciation. "That's what we do." He looked at me as he said it, so that I actually mumbled "okay." Thankfully I was drowned out by Petraeus.

"We only have 1.3 million active service members, 800 thousand in reserve," said Petraeus.

"You can figure that out," said Trump.

"The combined NATO forces in that theater are a little less than—"

"U, S, troops," Trump emphasized each word. "We don't mention NATO." Again he stared at me.

Late in the campaign I had carried his message into the black community, which some analysts credited with denying Clinton just enough votes to throw the election into chaos. My message had boiled down to: "Lower immigration means employers will need to hire more locals at higher wages." Trump heard about what I said, liked it, and must have decided I would always say the right thing, because I was now free to report out, uncensored.

Sitting against the wall in the White House situation room, I jotted down, *America ready to go it alone to protect its allies.*

"Of course we'll take the lead," said Petraeus.

"I don't care if anyone follows," said Trump. "Do we need them? Europe's a mess. They can't control their own borders, why do you think they can take care of someone else's?"

"So true," said Homeland Security Secretary Chris Christie.

"Point well taken," said Gingrich. "Donald's right, the last thing we need right now is Merkel and Hollande squabbling over turf. One million is our number."

Petraeus's face became extremely pinched.

"Now let's consider the next obvious question," said Christie. "What do we tell Putin?"

Gingrich leaned back in his chair. "That's a question Donald and I will contemplate."

"Nothing," said Trump. We tell him nothing and put another half-million troops on the border of that other little country they invaded..."

"Now we're up to a million and a half troops?" said Petraeus.

"The Crimea," said Gingrich. "Eastern Ukraine. Moldova and Romania might welcome us, as well."

"And then we put another half-million—give or take," he sourly said for Petraeus's benefit, "on his south border, in Turkey or Iraq, whichever is easiest."

"Good Lord," said Petraeus.

Trump looked at the others at the table, *Can you believe this guy?* Then he leaned toward Petraeus and thudded a finger on the table. "Don't go emailing your sweetheart about our plans, okay?"

A descending line of white met a rising wave of red below Petraeus's eyes. "Besides the fact that neither of those countries border Russia—"

"Close enough," said Trump, "Putin will get the point."

"We also don't have any basing rights in Iraq or Turkey."

"Did I say anything about a base? I want troops there. I want troops in the Middle East. Okay?" Trump said to the group. "We're good?" He stood, straightened his suit jacket and strode for the door. "How soon can we have the troops in those 3 places? How soon? Monday I hope. I think it should be Monday." He opened the door and motioned for me to leave with him. "That's what we're going to tell everybody. Don't make a liar out of me."

That night I played back the meeting to my wife. She liked everything she heard. "I hope the 2 million troops includes nukes."

Bel is what I call the nouveau black Republican, socially conservative and fiercely protective of our cities. Trump might be paying lip service to social values, but he seems true-blue on bringing jobs back to our cities.

We're from Detroit. The Motor City renaissance you've heard so much about? It's bull. The place is a soul-crushing post-apocalyptic dead zone.

But the day the Imperfect Compromise was made, and Trump was picked to go first? Two private equity funds announced plans to invest in Detroit. They said they're confident Trump can restart manufacturing. Whether their confidence comes from what Trump said during the campaign or what they may have heard privately, I don't know.

"Nuclear war is probably tomorrow's announcement," I said.

"I'm ready for it," said Bel. She exchanged her iPad for her sleep apnea mask and snuggled under the covers. "I doubt the Russian nukes will even detonate."

WELCOME TO THE HOTEL SOFITEL

SUNDAY WAS JUST SATURDAY EXTENDED for Petraeus, Joint Chiefs of Staff Chairman Joe Dunford and his generals as they scrambled to mobilize 2 million men and women, give or take. Trump micromanaged, receiving deployment stats every 30 minutes. He canceled all other meetings, despite the CIA, the FBI and the NSC ringing code-red terrorist alarms. He sat at a desk in the penthouse suite at the Lafayette Square Sofitel hotel a block from the White House, giving me an earful in between briefings from Petraeus's runners.

He had in front of him a placard with military burn rates by service and division. For instance an Army armored division cost the US Treasury $2 billion a week to deploy.

"If we wrap this up by March 1st," said Trump, "it'll be the cheapest war in history, adjusted for inflation." He was good with numbers.

"A good deal for the taxpayers," I volunteered.

"A great deal," he corrected. "Debt financing. That's the secret to a good deal. Load it up with debt. It might as well be off the books. Free money. Interest rates below inflation. Now's the time to make a deal."

"And we liberate the Lithuanians," said Vice President Elizabeth Warren. That was part of the Imperfect Compromise. Running mates were cast aside, and one half of the presidency got to name the other half's VP.

"A lot of Russians in Lithuania," said Trump. "Putin fans. I was looking to invest in a Black Sea resort in Georgia. All the hotel managers were Russians. They weren't Gorbachev or Yeltsin Russians, let me tell you. They knew how to get things done."

"Cronyism and intimidation can never be rewarded," said Warren. She had a hard time looking at Trump. It appeared that he was not the type of person she was accustomed to being around.

"Tell that to your pal Hillary," said Trump. "If she followed your rules, she would have to hand over the keys to Bernie. What a crime. I know the DNC's hack job on behalf of Hillary nearly killed Bernie. Really destroyed him."

"Bernie Sanders is proud to have played a key role in opening Hillary's eyes to the importance of social justice."

"There's only one person Hillary looks out for," said Trump. "You better watch your back."

Warren's spine stiffened. "Are you threatening me?"

Trump looked at me. "Is Wild Eyes for real?" That was his latest label for Warren. "She can't be that naïve, can she? It's good advice, Wild Eyes. I don't have to kill people, because I treat them fairly. I beat them, fairly."

Warren set her jaw and glared at the back of the couch. "Fair is a poor substitute for justice."

Trump frowned. "I have no idea what that means."

Warren trembled looking him in the eye. "You're going to start World War III, aren't you?"

"We're already *at* war. I'm going to finish it. That's what your side doesn't get."

Warren looked hurt. "I'm *your* VP, remember."

Secretary of State Gingrich had just walked in the room. "That happened quicker than I expected." He sat in front of Trump's desk. "I have a stack of calls to be returned. And an open chair at the NATO meeting this afternoon in Bonn."

"Good."

"The *Wall Street Journal* editorial called us 'simultaneously bellicose and rudderless.'"

"Good."

"The *Post's* afternoon edition has your face on page 1 with the headline, 'Chickenshit.'"

Trump didn't go so far as to say *good*, but he wasn't overly perturbed.

Gingrich glanced at Warren standing awkwardly a few feet away before asking the president, "So what's next?"

Trump pointed at him. "No one fires a shot or moves across those borders. We wait."

"We wait," said Warren in disgust and disbelief.

"First I'm too aggressive," said Trump, "and now I'm not aggressive enough? Make up your mind, Wild Eyes."

Warren headed for the door. "You're just terrible."

"Go tell Hillary all about it."

"Just terrible," Warren repeated.

"I like politicians with sex appeal," said Trump after she left the room. "Left or right. They gotta have sex appeal. I can't stand Wild Eyes."

"That explains why you love me," said Gingrich.

Trump smirked. "Are we getting any pushback in Ukraine and the Middle East?"

"Plenty," said Gingrich. "Mostly verbal. Some skirmishes with the Iranian Revolutionary Guard who operating in Iraq. We see it as good opportunities to thin their ranks."

"Keep building. Don't let Petraeus stop till we hit 2 million."

"The generals are all in," said Gingrich. "Deployment and planning are in full swing."

"Good. But no attacks."

"Nope."

"Anything else?"

Gingrich grimaced. "No one in your administration is on the same page. Our messaging is all over the board. Leaks springing up everywhere on the hull, all of them contradicting each other."

Trump looked at me.

Being around him made me bolder than I thought I could be. I went way beyond my job description, and capability. "You want me to start plugging them?"

"No," said Trump. "This is how you go unpredictable."

At noon Trump held a press briefing. He said not a word about the war brewing in the Baltics and ignored every question on the topic. Instead he talked about the wall.

"Tomorrow I'm calling up half a million reservists and sending them south to build the wall on our Mexican border. Congress doesn't get to approve it, this is self-defense, it's a military maneuver. I don't care what Congress thinks, we're building it. I said I would do it and I meant it.

"I've also started negotiations with the president of Mexico. Basically and not to give away our stance, but they're either paying for the wall or we're canceling NAFTA. Which is the worst trade deal in the history of the world. So don't worry, we'll get a good deal, I promise you.

"Now for the people who are here illegally, I tell you this. You better go home *now*. I'm not going to tell you again.

"If you want to get legal, turn yourself in. If you pass the checks, we'll see what we can do.

"I'm not going to go round you up, I don't have the time for that right now.

"But if you don't come see us, and you don't go back home…once that wall is up and we find you? That's going to be very bad for you. We're going to treat you like the national security threat that you are. We're going to put you in Guantanamo Bay and leave you there. Dad, Mom, the children, I don't care. It doesn't matter. It doesn't matter. You're a threat, everyone knows it.

"At some point, years down the road, maybe we'll put you on a boat and drop you off in South America. I don't know.

"But you won't be safe here. You make *us* less safe, I'm making *you* less safe. Very, very much less safe.

"For our reservists, we're going to take very good care of you. Great care of you. You're going to make more than you're making at your jobs, I can promise you that. When you're done building the wall, maybe you can help escort the criminals to Guantanamo. I don't know. Maybe we'll need you overseas. We'll see.

"Thank you."

DIRTY DOMESTIC

DISASTER

TRUMP HOSTED AN NFL PLAYOFF party at the Lafayette (no one called it the Sofitel). He wasn't comfortable in the White House. His wife and kids were, so we didn't see them much.

The invite list was long, the attendance thin. The party started in the ballroom; people bunched along the walls, leaving the center floor open and no one with a good sightline to the giant screen hung from the ceiling. Trump was nowhere to be found; early in the game, Homeland Secretary Christie grabbed a tray of appetizers and led the party upstairs to Trump's suite.

Now the room was full and the television was on the small side. It didn't matter, very few people were into it.

"First quarter total points, 9, odd, that's another point for me," Attorney General Ted Cruz crowed.

"Ted," said former Minnesota governor Norm Coleman, "you're the only guy I know who's excited about coming in first in the pool while your team loses the game."

It was true, the Cowboys were down 9-0 to the Vikings in the NFC championship game. (That these teams were vying for a Super Bowl berth was testimony to the damage the One Person One Vote protest movement had done to the NFL.)

"Say the word, Ted," said Vegas kingpin Steve Winn. "A couple phone calls and I can guarantee you win our pool; but the Cowboys get crushed."

Cruz gave them both a cold smile. "I only know how to play the game one way, gentlemen. Principled."

"Honey," Bel urgently tugged me toward the TV screen. As a diehard Lions fan, she hated both these teams and so was the only person watching the game, looking for validation the winner would be crushed in the

Super Bowl. She pointed. "What's happening?"

My first impression was that I was seeing a choreographed halftime show, as if the crowd was holding up purple signs in an outward-spreading circle. But it was in fact a panicked emptying of the seats, people fleeing down and over the rows. They ran away from a central point—the camera zoomed in on a man alone in the middle of the vacated section, and then the screen flashed white and the TV speakers rumbled with what sounded like thunder.

"Oh no," said Norm Coleman.

The camera regained focus. There was now a gaping hole which grew by the instant as the stands collapsed. The announcers were panicked and then they were screaming, briefly, before the screen went dark and silent.

"Turn to CNN," said Bel.

Someone did and an aerial shot showed smoke pouring out of the brand-new glass-walled stadium into the frigid air. People streamed into the surrounding streets.

One side of the stadium collapsed.

"Code yellow?" Christie said into his phone. "Confirm code yellow."

"What's that mean?" said Bel.

Christie covered his ear to listen to the phone. "Get me a reading! Is it dirty? … Radiation or germ? … How do we know it's not both? … Shit…" He hurried out of the room.

The CNN coverage cut to a camera inside a stadium concourse. Pure pandemonium. People ran and slammed into each other and stampeded security personnel attempting to control access to the escalator.

They cut back to the aerial view, starting tight on one of the exits and panning back. Cops, fire trucks, ambulances, bomb vans, they were encircling the stadium at a 2-block perimeter. Emergency personnel fanned out, trying to funnel people into a handful of white semi-trailers.

This was mostly unsuccessful. People broke free of these cordons, running down city streets, into neighborhoods, over bridges spanning intersecting interstates and the Mississippi River. They slipped and fell on the ice. Sirens screamed and bullhorn-voices gave orders. Gunfire popped every few seconds.

Half our room had run out. The rest were on their phone, talking, texting, searching.

"Nate and Jen are at the game," said Bel. Her brother and his wife. She looked at her phone like it held terrible news. I led her to the couch.

"They'll let us know they're okay as soon as they can," I said. My government-issue phone buzzed. "He's paging me. Can you sit tight? I don't want you out there right now. Stay here, okay?" I kissed Bel and went to find Trump.

BIPARTISAN GOVERNANCE

A SUICIDE BOMBER HAD DETONATED A radioactive "dirty" bomb in the stadium. Wires had been crossed and many authorities onsite and across the country thought it was anthrax or some other airborne microbe. They had attempted to quarantine those fleeing, potentially exposing them to additional radiation.

The stadium, between the massive explosion and the radiation, was ruined. So too potentially was everything within a half-mile radius. That included 2 new Wells Fargo office towers, scores of businesses and thousands of condos and townhomes in the redeveloping east end of downtown Minneapolis.

Guns had made it into the stadium, guns had been drawn by citizens intent on leaving, and by police attempting the quarantine and dragnetting for terrorists, causing an as-yet unknown number of casualties.

Trump's national security team sequestered in a hardened D.C. site as a precaution and an evasion of the press, ensuring all information and rumors traveled one way, in. By 6 a.m. Monday we still had no definitive word of the identity and backing of the terrorists.

"I don't care who it was," said Trump. "Now we go after ISIS."

Gingrich steepled his fingers. For a roomful of old guys after a sleepless 24 hours, they all looked sharp. "How?" Judging by the silent communication around the table, he was asking on behalf of Defense Secretary Petraeus, who in turn was receiving looks from JCS Chairman Dunford.

"With our army," said Trump. "Troops. Boots on the ground. We invade Syria, Iraq, Iran, Saudi Arabia, Turkey. All of them."

"Syria and Iraq should be sufficient," said Gingrich.

"If it wasn't ISIS," said Petraeus, "we have a Bush the Younger problem again."

"We?" said Trump. He and Petraeus did not like each other. "Which one of the 2 of us was elected?"

"To be accurate," said Petraeus, "neither of us."

Trump's eyes narrowed and his chin jutted forward. "Who employs who, Mr. Memoirs? One of us answers to the American people; and one of us answers to me."

They locked eyes; Trump was first to look away, at me. "Get me another latte."

Gingrich drew everyone's attention. "David, Joe, draw up a gameplan for Donald to review. Give him 3 very different options in terms of size and severity."

"We're stretched incredibly thin with our deployments in eastern Europe," said Petraeus. "It's going to limit what we can do vis-à-vis ISIS."

"I don't want limits, general," said Trump. "I want problem solving."

Petraeus nodded. "We have a buttload of allies, enemies and everything in between operating in the Middle Eastern theater. It's going to take cooperation."

"Leave that to us," said Gingrich. "Just assume we're going it alone for now, and tell us how many and how long it will take to get our forces in position."

"In the meantime we have to protect this country," said Trump, turning to Homeland Secretary Christie. "No more Muslims, Chris. No more in this country."

"Sure," said Christie. "Are we talking visas—"

"I'm talking no one. Not a tourist or a student. Not a father or a grandmother. None. N-o-n-e. And we wiretap and get rid of any suspicious Muslims already in this country. You got it?"

Christie sighed.

"Don't sigh," Trump ordered.

"Donald, what you're saying is impossible," said Christie.

"You're wrong. Do you understand me? Do all of you understand me?" Trump nodded at each person at the table, encouraging them to give him a return nod.

Christie looked hangdog, which should have been shocking to see from the brash former prosecutor. But we had all seen it a few times already. Christie was either intimidated by the man above him or loathing himself for accepting such a position.

"I'm just letting you know," said Christie, "we're going to have every interest group on the right and left tearing us a new one on this."

"I don't care. I think you're wrong, very wrong. People are scared."

"Maybe we get some help from Congress on this one?" said Christie.

"Are you kidding me?" said Trump.

Congress by the way was Democrat in the Senate 51–49 and Republican in the House by a similar slim margin.

"That's not possible," Trump chewed out Christie, "and it's not what the people want. They want action. They're okay with debate *after* action has been taken. That's the way it works."

Elizabeth Warren crossed her arms. "Chris is right. You can't do that."

"Watch me," said Trump.

She looked at Attorney General Cruz, who was taking it all in without any change in facial expression. "Perhaps you have an opinion, Ted?"

"Until I do the research," said Cruz, "I only have facts. And that is, presidents can do whatever they want until the courts tell them to stop."

"You both satisfied?" Trump asked Warren and Christie.

"Oh completely," Warren heaped on the sarcasm.

Petraeus was uncomfortable in his chair. "If you'll excuse us, General Dunford and my time is better spent with our staffs."

"Go." Trump waved them away.

I left the room with them to go get that latte.

The Minneapolis bombing claimed 256 lives and another 1,100 or so people injured. Perhaps another 120,000 people in the stadium and the surrounding area had been exposed to varying degrees of potentially harmful radiation. Amid comparisons to Chernobyl, downtown Minneapolis became an instant ghost town. In advance of a forecast for strong westerly winds Tuesday, the University of Minnesota campus was vacated as well.

Panic lived across the country as no one could offer any assurance the next dirty bomb could be stopped. Over the course of the week the stock market dropped another 2,000 points, sunk to its lowest moment of the 2008 Great Recession. The Super Bowl was postponed; eventually it would be canceled.

Attendance plummeted at sporting events, concerts, expos. Trump, Christie and the national security team spent all of Monday trading briefings with law enforcement officials from the country's major cities, focusing on the risks to the D.C. political complex and the Manhattan financial center.

On Tuesday the 4 congressional leaders gathered in Trump's hotel suite. "First of all," said Trump, "I want to tell you everything is under control."

"I'd say it's anything but," said House Minority Leader Nancy Pelosi.

"It's a free country," said Trump, looking more apt to have Pelosi escorted out than humor her 1st Amendment rights. "I didn't bring you here to convince you of anything. That's not my job as commander in chief. My job is to make a deal for the American people."

"You did campaign as dealmaker-in-chief," said Speaker of the House Paul Ryan. "So what's the deal? What do you have for us? Free tuition at your university in exchange for a higher wall?"

"Don't show off for your buddies, okay Paul? Don't be crass. That's not how we do it around here."

"Okay Donald," said Senate Minority Leader Mitch McConnell. "What do you want from us?"

"I want to give you the chance to actually participate in government. I want a tax deal. What do you have for me?"

Senate Majority Leader Dick Durbin was puzzled. "What do we have for *you*?"

"I know what I want," said Trump unkindly. "What do you want? Surely you have a wish list a mile long after all these years."

Ryan chuckled. "It doesn't work that way, Donald."

Trump stared at each of the 4 in turn. "Then why would you even come to the table?"

Pelosi cocked her head. "I want the minimum wage increased to $15 an hour."

Trump shook his head. "Nope. Wages will go up when we plug all the immigration holes and stop China from cheating us. How about student loan debt? Ivanka had a great idea. Since we have all these kids with loans—"

"Whoa, hang on, Donald," said McConnell. "Let's not turn over policymaking to your daughter and Chelsea Clinton."

Trump slowly shook his head. He seemed to disengage from the discussion. "So tell me what you want."

Ryan gave a look to his legislative brethren and leaned forward elbows on knees. "We all have a lot on our plates right now, with the foreign engagements and domestic terrorism. We'll have our staffs pull together a legislative priorities list, and you have your team create a rough budget framework."

"I've already decided what we're going to do," said Trump. "We can budget for it later."

"It doesn't work that way," said Ryan.

"You put a budget forward," said Pelosi, "and the Republicans in the House draft the legislation. *Then* we can start negotiating toward a deal."

"Are you teaching me how deal-making works?" Trump demanded. "Your way hasn't worked in decades. The people don't have time for that."

"Donald," said McConnell, "I know you're in a rush with only 6 months—"

"This isn't a rush," said Trump. "You should see me in a rush. I didn't run for president to play the Washington game. I ran to save the country."

McConnell squinched his eyes. "I'm afraid the populism mantle needed to be removed when you took office."

Trump stood up and pointed to the door. "If you're not going to work with me, I'll fix things myself. Maybe after they finally vote you out of office, you'll even like what I'm going to do."

"No one has stopped working with you," said Ryan.

Trump shook his head. "I'll go it alone."

"On taxes?" said Ryan. "You can't. That's not within the executive prerogative."

"It's a lot bigger than you think," said Trump. "When's the last time the courts ruled consistently according to your definition of executive prerogative?"

The legislators were seething, McConnell most of all. He took a half-step toward Trump. "Don't you dare make a mockery of our hallowed system."

Trump gave them a dismissive wave. "I'll give you till Friday. Not 1 or 2 of you, not just the Republicans or Democrats. All 4 of you. Otherwise the next time you come to the table, you won't have a chair."

GOING IT ALONE

WEDNESDAY JANUARY 25TH, THE RUSSIANS made their move. As in the Crimea and eastern Ukraine, they claimed only to be aiding a repressed Russian ethnic minority assert their rights. But this time they made no attempt to mask the Russian insignia on the tanks and other war machines.

Reports put the initial Lithuanian casualty count at 82 dead and scores more severely wounded. Lithuanian president Grybauskaitė begged for NATO assistance. The US issued no official response while continuing the unilateral troop build-up. Germany, France and the U.K. complained bitterly about the US while arguing amongst themselves and internally over how many troops to commit.

The UN called for the establishment of a humanitarian corridor to ensure safe transit for Lithuania's panicked non-ethnic Russians fleeing west. NATO agreed but by the end of the week, without US leadership, hadn't figured out how to make it happen.

Trump held a press conference Saturday morning on the White House lawn while reports were coming in about a US ground force moving into northern Iraq and Syria.

"I've been criticized for not taking questions from our esteemed media since I took office just over a week ago," he began. "Meanwhile Hillary hasn't held a press conference for *years*. *Years*. But that's okay. I'm very happy to oblige. Fire away."

A *Washington Post* reporter went first. "Are we invading the countries of Iraq and Syria?"

"If you want to call them countries, sure. I'm not so sure."

"We are invading them?"

"Yes."

"Could you elaborate?"

"We are going to eliminate the Islamic State," said Trump. "Obama and Hillary Clinton were too afraid to engage them. I'm not. Real Americans aren't afraid. This is what our military trains for. Frankly it's going to be a slaughter. We are going to *slaughter* the radical Islamic terrorists the same way they want to slaughter us."

"There are reports," said a *New York Times* reporter, "that the attack on Minneapolis was perhaps organized and executed by a Kurdish faction, and that their motivation—"

"I'm cutting you off right there," said Trump. "I know what you're going to say. That we're somehow responsible for Turkey bombing the hell out of the Kurds. First of all, that was Obama who left the Kurds hanging out to dry, okay? Second, if we find out it was the Kurds who attacked us, they'll pay too, alright? This time maybe it was the Kurds, the next time it's ISIS, then it's Iran."

A Fox News reporter jumped in. "Are you saying we would invade Iran as well?"

Trump put his chin forward. "Whatever it takes. Whatever it takes. Speaking of which, does anyone want to hear about what we're doing to fix the broken economy?"

"Why not," said the Fox reporter.

Trump gripped the lectern. "I won't even make you ask that in the form of a question. We're doing 4 things—actually we're going to do a *lot* of things, let me tell you. I'll tell you 4 of them now. And let me just say, I tried to work with Congress on this. But they have more important things to do. Like thinking about the 2018 elections."

This got a twitter from the press corps.

"First of all," said Trump, "as I promised in the campaign, it's time to make China pay for their currency manipulation. So, starting tomorrow, we are fining every Chinese import. The fine will be equal the amount they're cheating on each item."

"Can you define how they're cheating?" asked a Bloomberg reporter.

"You know how, everyone knows," said Trump. "They're cheating by deflating their currency. Which makes their goods cheaper here. Which destroys jobs because our companies can't produce that cheaply. What-ever the Chinese currency *should* cost, that's what the Chinese product is *going* to cost.

"Second, we're going to fine the products that US companies make in overseas factories and import back into the US. Ford comes to mind.

They decided to build their electric cars in Mexico." He pointed in a direction somewhere between Detroit and Mexico. "They're cheating, same as the Chinese, by using cheap Mexican labor. Then they sell it here and the car companies building cars here can't compete, they can't make the product here as cheaply. And so we lose even more jobs.

"Both of these fines—and they are fines, not duties or taxes, so Congress doesn't get to mess this up. We're going to put these fines, this money, in a fund. It's not going to the US government, let me tell you. No. The fund goes to US companies who decide to build these products *here*. It's going to allow them to be able to employ people at *great* wages. This is huge for jobs, let me tell you.

"Third, we're reducing interest rates. Not a little reduction. Not a quarter point now, and maybe a quarter point in another few months," he mocked that approach. "We're knocking them down a full percentage point. Negative, that makes them negative. The Federal Reserve is on board.

"Fourth, and this is a big one. We're eliminating the income tax. Effective January first. Not next January. *This* January first. Twenty-some days ago." Trump waved off all the hands raised and questions shouted. "In its place we'll have a sales tax. That will start April first. So if you have any big purchases you're thinking about, I suggest you do it now. Individuals, companies, everyone.

"And don't worry, the new sales tax isn't going to be that big. Fifteen percent maybe? We'll start small and only increase it if we need to. So you don't have to worry about buying everything now. It still won't cost that much, okay?"

He acknowledged a *Slate* reporter.

"Have you received Congress's input?"

"I haven't and I'll tell you why. The income tax system is the single biggest corrupting influence in America. Congress's ability to sell changes to the income tax code leads to huge political donations. It's Congress's most powerful weapon to extract campaign contributions. Not to make America better. Just to stay in office. It's the most corrupt system. So do you think Congress wants me to do this? The answer is no."

An AP reporter went next. "Is there any significance to a new national sales tax starting on April Fool's Day?"

Trump scowled. "We'll make it effective on the second, fine."

Reporters were looking at each other, unsure how to ask a question that wouldn't sound as if they were condoning what they clearly viewed as insanity. "On the new sales tax, will there be an exemption to protect lower income people?" said an NBC reporter.

"They're not currently paying any income taxes," said Trump. He paused, lower lip protruding. "Okay, sure." He looked at an attractive BBC America reporter. "These have been great questions. Really. Let's hear what our friends the Brits want to know."

Disappointingly, she did not have a British accent. "Is anything you're doing constitutional?"

"*That's* what Britain wants to know? Really?" Trump looked disgusted, disinterested in the topic. "Raising taxes, lowering taxes. What's unconstitutional? We do it all the time. I run the IRS, they do what I tell them to do. The people, let me tell you this, the *people* will love this. *Every* body. Okay? It should have been done a long, long time ago. Now we're doing it and it's going to save the country and everybody is going to love what I'm doing."

"Can you tell us why you're doing this?" asked the *NYT* reporter.

"Listen to this guy," Trump attempted to enlist the rest of the media to his side. "Like I don't have a reason? Like I'm just making this up? Jobs, okay? That's what people care about. Having a *job*. That's all. Everything else is second. Ninety-nine percent of the country is happy if they have a job."

"And that's what these policies are intended to do?"

Trump held up his hands and looked around incredulously. "Yes? Yes? Yes, that's why we're taking *action. Action*, not *policies*. Democrats have policies. Republicans too. I don't like policies, I have to tell you. I'm a fan of action." He smirked at the *NYT* reporter. "I know that's going to take some getting used to."

That afternoon I ran an errand to the White House for Donald. In the 2nd floor hallway of the West Wing, Elizabeth Warren stood in the doorway to her office. I nodded to her in passing.

"Do you have a moment?"

"Not really…"

It felt like an offer I shouldn't refuse. She welcomed me into her office and shut the door. "On the run for your boss?" Warren studied me. "Don't you think it's odd he refuses to spend any time over here? It worries me that our nation's business is being conducted in a hotel room. It feels like he has things to hide."

I shrugged. "You're always welcome over there."

"Welcome? I doubt that. Do you feel welcome there?"

"Sure. As much as anyone."

"After everything he said about Hispanics and Muslims?"

"Maybe if I was either of them."

"It doesn't bother you he's a racist?"

"I haven't noticed. Of course maybe he's careful around his black employees."

Warren retreated behind her desk. "I don't feel comfortable around him. He's a misogynist, that you can't argue. I thought maybe you could empathize with me."

"Sympathize, I guess."

Warren soured her lips. "I need to know how bad things are going to get. Who's he going to nominate for the Supreme Court?"

"I have no idea."

"It's Ted Cruz, isn't it?"

I was uncomfortable. But she was part of the administration. What she chose to do with the information was up to her and her conscience. And Trump honestly didn't seem to care who knew what. "I think so." Cruz had been lobbying hard for it, that was what I was hearing.

"That would be a disaster," said Warren. "You know that, right?" she asked when I didn't react. "He's probably more racist than Trump, if that's possible. He pretends to be a champion of the Constitution, but you and I both know Ted Cruz is nothing but a rabid conservative." She raised her eyebrows, waiting for me to agree, or at least respond.

"I know you feel that way," I finally said.

Warren came around to sit on the corner of her desk in front of me. "You can speak freely here. I would never divulge anything confidential or sensitive. If you know of anything that could possibly jeopardize the security of this country, it's your obligation as an American citizen to bring it to light. I'm very afraid, understandably afraid, about this man doing irreparable damage to our way of life. Don't you agree?"

I squirmed. "I really need to get going."

Warren stared at me and shook her head, pity on her face. "Okay, go back to doing his bidding."

She did a great job making it feel like I was the Devil's slave.

FOREIGN POLICY

T HE MOST INCREDIBLE MEETING I'VE ever witnessed took place 4 days later on February 1st. Trump called me at 3:30 a.m. and had me meet him at the Lafayette. I'm a morning person, this was only 45 minutes before my normal wake-up. Still, I didn't have time to shit, shave or shower. So I was a little discombobulated when I walked into his suite and was introduced to Vladimir Putin.

It was just me, Trump, Donald Jr., and Putin.

Trump had come to trust me, maybe more than anyone else in his administration. As evidence of that, I think I'm the only one in the administration or on staff who made his kids jealous.

"This one doesn't come out until you publish your memoirs," Trump told me. The first and only censoring of my communications.

Putin was in a linen suit, silk shirt 3 buttons open, no socks. He sat down gracefully, crossed one leg over the other and sipped what appeared to be a vodka martini, no olive. "I trust you didn't ask me here to push the 'reset button.'"

Don Jr. chuckled. He glanced at his father before speaking. "First there has to *be* a relationship, am I right, Vlad? That's why we're here."

Putin's eyes flickered back and forth between the Trumps. I feel like he thought he was Daniel Craig as James Bond. "I've been up since 5 a.m. Moscow time, yesterday. I don't know I have the stamina to build a relationship."

Trump tugged at his buttoned-up collar. "I've done very good deals for both parties with very little relationship."

"And preferably with very little sleep for the other party," said Putin with a humorless smile.

Trump flipped his hands unhappily and settled back in his chair. "No one sleeps much."

Putin shrugged but every-so-slightly shifted forward. "So what would you like from me?"

Trump gave his son the green light with a nod. Don Jr. took time gathering his thoughts. "We would like a way to move our troops off the Crimean border."

Putin spread his hands. "If you need a lift, we would be happy to help."

Don Jr.'s eyes widened. Trump Sr. reengaged. "As long as you're offering. Take us south down the Black Sea. Half a million men and a lot of firepower. It'll take many ships."

Putin's expression froze for a beat. An eyebrow twitched. "You are serious."

"We're serious about defeating extremism," said Don Jr.

Putin's eyes remained lidded but there was excitement underneath. "There is nothing extreme about what we are doing in the Baltics. That is historic Russia."

"There needs to be a boundary," said Trump.

"We have one," said Putin. "We can show you. It's not unreasonable."

"There will need to be compensation paid for any lost assets," said Don Jr. "Public and private. And humanitarian assistance."

"We will need to be paid for the…" Putin searched for the right word. "…taxi service."

Trump spread his hands. "We already paid to mobilize all these troops."

Putin shrugged. "How does that compensate *us*?"

Don Jr. leaned in. "When you transport our troops safely and effectively to the Middle East, and make clear that you are stopping at your prescribed boundary, we'll withdraw the troops from the Lithuanian border."

"That's a great, great value to you," said Trump.

Putin pondered it. "And Russia's interests in the Middle East?"

"I don't think you have much at stake there," said Trump. "A lot to lose."

Putin neither accepted or refuted that.

"For us it's security," said Trump.

"And oil," said Putin.

Trump shrugged. "We'll get paid."

"You know that oil is not such a big deal for us anymore," said Don Jr. "It's a big deal for you. Anything we do in the Middle East will increase prices. That makes our domestic producers happy. And it makes you happy."

Putin regarded the Trumps. "That is your goal? A happy Russia."

"Our goal," said Trump, "is not to care about you. Crimea, Ukraine, Lithuania, nobody in the US cares. Not really. If you keep it that way, we can pull back those troops."

Putin stood. "I will consider your offer." They shook hands; it appeared to be a grip test. "Assad must stay."

"As long as he likes," said Trump. "Of course there isn't going to be much left to rule."

THE BLACK
COMMUNITY

CONGRESS SCREAMED. DEMOCRAT AND REPUBLICAN alike. About absolutely everything Trump was doing. Press conferences were sparsely attended, because there were just so many, the media was stretched so thin. Lawsuits were filed, injunctions requested, inquiries promised. But Trump plunged forward. And very few outside of Congress seemed to object.

My job description included frequent visits to the "black community." It gave Bel and me opportunities to go back to Detroit. If you've been there lately, you'll understand why we sometimes chose to go to Chicago.

Our first visit, we allowed a handful of community support organizations to pull together and conduct the meeting. Remember I said "very few" people were complaining about Trump...

"What this usurper is doing makes a mockery of the principles of justice upon which this country was founded!" thundered one of the organizers at the meeting. "This would-be dictator is shredding our social fabric and devolving America into a 3rd-world banana republic. He has turned his back on this community! Where is the attention to police reform, judicial reform, and community investment? In *Trump's* world, *our* world is made to disappear, swept under the rug and trampled upon. And Congress sits back and lets it happen, convening kangaroo courts to kowtow to the man who would be not a president but a king!"

That was a small portion of his preamble, before opening the floor to questions. The questions I received were mostly complaints and requests for assistance. I didn't stay long and I didn't bother giving Trump much feedback, he wouldn't have listened.

I didn't formally announce our 2nd trip. Instead I asked my pastor to work with his peers to put together an informal discussion group. It took place a few days after construction started on the Mexican wall, with interest rates pushed negative, the income tax eliminated, Russia enabled, war waged in the Middle East, and Muslims banned from entering the country.

(And spied on if they were already in. Trump personally wanted to be able to eavesdrop on anybody in the country, if not anybody in the world. As he put it, "If they aren't bad guys, they won't care.")

In the basement of the First Methodist church in front of 56 black men and women, I introduced myself as a member of the Trump team and received a standing ovation.

"Your man came to get things *done!*" said one gentleman.

"And I'm not sure I even care what it is," added a lady. "It just feels good to have something happening!"

"He closed the border, that's what," said another lady. "Slammed it shut. They pay $6 an hour at the mega-store down the street. They say they pay $12. They post jobs at $12. But no one ever gets one of those. Because the illegals are working for $6 without benefits. That's gonna *end.*"

A big dude stood up at the end of the session and addressed me directly. "I have a list of 23 illegals in our neighborhood. I'll give it to you to give to Trump."

I didn't give Trump that list, and I didn't give him much of that feedback either, he didn't need any encouragement.

TURNOVER

O N FRIDAY FEBRUARY 17TH, VLADIMIR Putin called Trump to accept the offer. Trump alerted Defense Secretary Petraeus and instructed him to coordinate troop transports with his Russian counterpart.

To celebrate the deal, Trump invited Bel and me to join him, Melania and Ivanka for a drink.

We sat around a coffee table in tightly-upholstered high-backed chairs in the drawing room of his Lafayette suite.

It was Bel who proposed the first toast. "To the best 1st month in presidential history."

I was slower than everyone else putting champagne flutes into the middle for clinking. Ivanka gave me a piercing look.

"What a month," I said, eyes on the clinking glasses.

"To the final days of Islamic extremism," Ivanka toasted before I had a chance to sip on the first one. "And the security that will soon follow." This time I was quicker to the clink.

"In all honesty," I said, "no matter what one thinks of your ideology, they can't argue this: you're a man who gets things done."

No one hoisted a flute. "Ideology has this country tied in knots," said Melania. "You can found a country on ideology, but you run it to optimize your people's success."

"If I relied on ideology," said Trump, "I wouldn't have made billions of dollars and I wouldn't be President of the United States."

"Sometimes I wish you weren't," said Melania, sounding tired but maintaining great posture. "I think the stress has already aged you 10 years."

"I was amazed at how youthful Putin looks," I said.

Trump nodded. "He takes good care of himself."

"Bel," I said with all the sincerity I could muster, "I've been trying to tell you for years. The secret is a morning martini."

Everyone laughed. "Yes, he did," said Trump. "But always remember,

Russians can hold their liquor."

Melania touched Bel's knee. "How are you holding up as a neglected Washington spouse?"

"I love it," said Bel. "He worked all the time anyway. The kids and I are used to it. We're really enjoying the city. It's a wonderful change of pace."

"I feel so sorry for Detroit," said Ivanka.

"We're gonna bring it back," said Trump. "Eric has acquired some great, great properties there. We're going to build, build, build."

I exchanged a glance with Ivanka. "There's no conflict of interest," she said. "Eric is having our portfolio manager do all the work. We're *investing* in our cities. And not just in Detroit."

"*Every* city abandoned by our politicians," said Trump.

Bel raised her glass. "To the rebirth of our cities."

A knock at the door competed with the high-quality crystal clinking. Newt Gingrich entered and stared at Trump. "Can I have a word?"

Trump motioned me to follow him into the main room.

Gingrich held a rolled-up sheaf of papers. He slapped it against his palm. "We have a deal with Putin?"

"You heard?"

"Petraeus is lining up Russian ships to transport our troops."

"Good. That's what I told him to do."

"Donald…" Gingrich was incredulous. "Why didn't you ask me?"

"Because I was dealing with Putin. Not your peer."

"I'm talking about the *strategy*. About the *intelligence* of what we're doing. There is none, Donald." The men were face to face, Gingrich's voice edging higher. Ivanka stood in the doorway listening. "Putin took you to the woodshed."

Trump's eyes narrowed. "It's a great deal, Newt."

"For Russia. Not for Europe. Not for the Baltics."

"A lot of Russians there would tell you different. A lot."

"No, most of them wouldn't. Do you know what's going to happen? Putin is going to attempt to create a corridor connecting Kaliningrad with Russia proper. That will cut the Baltics in half like an Iron Curtain, and take us back to the 1950's."

"The 1950's were very stable, very profitable," said Trump. Gingrich looked stunned. Trump's confidence appeared to waver. "You and I both know those boundaries are historically artificial."

"They're called borders, not boundaries," Gingrich's voice overrode Trump's. "And borders are sacrosanct. If they're breached, we either have a dramatic tilt toward Russian-Chinese hegemony…or we have World War III."

Trump nodded, shook his head, paced to the side, and returned to stand in front of Gingrich, looking pugilistic. "So you need to make sure that doesn't happen."

"No." Gingrich gazed at the door. "I'm not going to own this. You didn't consult me. I'm not going to be responsible for what happens. In fact, I'm going to do what I can to stop it. From the outside."

"You're quitting?"

"I resign effective immediately."

Trump glared and pointed at the door. "I'll give you till 6 a.m. to reconsider."

"Don't bother setting your alarm." Gingrich walked out. "When this hits tomorrow's press, the cries of fear and rage will wake you."

Ivanka, Melania and Bel joined us. "That's the most gutless thing I've ever seen," said Trump's daughter.

"With everything he's been through," said Trump, "I didn't expect Newt to bail out at the first controversy."

"Do you even need a secretary of state?" said Melania. "I mean *really*, do you?"

"I make the deals," said Trump.

"You will need one," I said.

Looking a little lost, scanning the room as if searching for a list of candidates, Trump said, "I have a lot of very, very good people waiting for the opportunity."

THE CABINET

TRUMP CONVENED A STATUS MEETING with his cabinet and leadership team on Tuesday, February 21ˢᵗ. Sarah Palin, Energy Secretary, wanted to go first.

"Good morning everyone. I have lots of great news to report. First, we greenlighted the Keystone pipeline and the Dakota Access pipeline. Big hurray on that. We're also bringing suit in conjunction with the Interior department against various windfarms and solar fields for killing eagles—"

"Sarah. Please," said Trump. "Anything important to tell us?"

"Yes. We're going to approve 3 different plans for new nuclear energy—"

"Sarah, you are boring the people in this room. You are boring the President. We'll come back to you if there's time at the end of the meeting." Trump pointed at Christie. "Let's hear about our security."

"Energy *is* security," Palin grumbled to Health & Human Services director Ben Carson.

Christie came with much less energy than Palin. "Everything is coming along."

"Is the wall done?" said Trump.

"We're making progress," said Christie.

"Percent complete?"

Christie frowned. "I'll have to check."

Trump's eyes goggled. "You come to a status meeting without percent complete? Have you ever been to a development project status meeting? You'd be laughed out of the room, and probably off the project."

Christie wore a blank mask. "I'd say 20%."

"I've heard much lower," said Trump. "We have 6 months, Chris."

"I'm aware."

"Not 6 months to get it built," said Trump, "6 months to have it *working*. We can't give Hillary any opportunity to claim it's not functional."

"We'll be there."

"I'm also hearing bad things about airport security."

Christie squirmed. "Can we take that off line?"

"No."

Christie pondered what he wanted to say. "I think we have a plan to do this right."

"*Right?*"

"So that we don't run afoul of religious liberty."

"There's no such thing when it comes to national security," said Trump. "We decide who comes into our country."

"That's right," said Christie, "and we can't discriminate based on—"

"You're talking about hurting feelings," Trump cut him off. "That's not the guy I hired. And that's not what I ordered you to do."

Christie tried to weather the storm. "Again, I think we'd be better served taking this off line."

"Chris," said Cruz, "I can give you the cover you need legally. The last thing we need right now is a Muslim extremist who skated through security blowing up a school."

"That's much more likely to come from an anti-government radical who thinks the schools are leftist factories," said Christie.

Palin jumped out of her chair while Cruz said, "Oh Chris," but Trump kept Christie's attention. "Speaking of internal threats, how is the Muslim surveillance coming?"

"We've redoubled our efforts to work with the Muslim community—"

"Did I tell you to work with them?"

"Let me tell you," said Christie, "we're light years ahead of what Obama was doing."

"That's not what I promised." Trump stood. "'Better than Obama' is a joke, okay? I don't care if I'm here for 6 months or 8 years. No one says that ever again. Chris…" He pointed to the door.

"What?" Christie looked from door to Trump. "You're not…are you?"

Trump nodded. He went to some length not to say the words. "It's time."

"You're firing me?" Christie's arms flopped on the table. He didn't seem to have the strength to rise. "Donald, you know we could do a lot of great things together. Really great things."

"I thought so too. It never seemed to happen."

Christie got to his feet. "Okay." He looked around the table. "Everyone, I still have high hopes for what you can accomplish. Please take good care of this country." A nod to Trump and he was out the door.

"Looks like I have 2 positions to fill." Trump turned to Secretary of Defense Petraeus. "You want to interview for Secretary of State? Tell me how our international relations are going."

Petraeus had a slim briefing book open in front of him. "As you know, we encountered very few difficulties with the coordinated troop movements with the Russians. To my knowledge it was unprecedented cooperation between our militaries. Not to mention the Turks giving us passage to the Mediterranean and the Syrians keeping their mouths shut when we offloaded at Tartus."

"What did you learn about the Russians?" said Cruz.

"I'd say we came away impressed with the professionalism of their navy," said Petraeus. "And pleased at the obsolescence of their hardware."

"We can take them?" said Cruz.

"It's possible," said Petraeus, "that Putin held back his top stuff and only showed us what he wants us to believe. But not likely. It doesn't fit his psy-profile."

Trump winked happily at Cruz, who received it like Mr. Spock.

Petraeus was acing the interview. "Currently the Russians are consolidating their positions in Lithuania and Latvia. The theory of a planned corridor connecting these positions has been neither confirmed nor refuted at this point. If it does happen it will happen fast, so we need a planned response."

"How about ISIS?" said Trump.

Petraeus turned the page in his briefing book. "The reinforcements via the Black Sea had an impact. ISIS elements have withdrawn from a number of erstwhile strategic towns in northern Iraq and Syria. As we pursue them, we're coming into conflict with Iranians or their proxies."

"They shouldn't push us," said Trump. "We don't need much excuse."

"Regarding ISIS," said Petraeus, "it also appears a significant element is consolidating in Dabiq."

"That's very considerate of them," said Trump. "Can we safely bomb the hell out of it?"

"If by 'safely' you mean with few civilian casualties, I believe so. Dabiq has been under ISIS control for almost 2 years, there aren't many innocents remaining. But there's a theological aspect to consider."

"The fact that they are evil Islamic fascist nut-jobs," said Palin.

Petraeus didn't spare her a glance. "They reportedly believe scripture foretells a penultimate battle in Dabiq where the 'armies of Rome' are defeated. We are presumably the army of Rome. Although some say it's referencing Istanbul, as the former center of eastern Christianity. Coincidentally, Turkey is our most ardent ally. They're blasting away at ISIS, and taking the opportunity to drive out the Kurds."

"We can't let that happen," said Health Secretary Carson. "The Kurds are one of the few true allies we have there. I learned that when I visited the refugee camps."

"They shouldn't have bombed the Metrodome," said Palin.

"That wasn't the Metrodome," said Cruz. "And it wasn't the Kurds. That was Turkish propaganda."

"Short of going to war with Turkey," said Petraeus, "there's not a lot we can do about their engagement with the Kurds. And they are taking on ISIS at the same time."

"I don't care about the Kurds," said Trump. "I want ISIS. Bomb this town, Dubuque."

"Dabiq," said Petraeus. "If we do that it fits their end-of-times theology. And it might inspire a huge number of disaffected Muslims to join them."

"Good, let our Muslims go over there, then we can bomb them too," said Trump.

"There's also the chance," said Petraeus, "that al Qaeda could suddenly reconcile and join them. We should consider starving ISIS out. Make it anti-climactic."

"I don't want Iran thinking we're afraid to finish things," said Trump.

"We need to draw out Iran and expose the mullahs' true intentions toward Israel," said Cruz. "It's time to quit pretending sanctions and negotiations can work with madmen."

"Get ready," said Trump. "Tomorrow I tear up the deal Obama made on their nukes."

VP Elizabeth Warren exploded right out of her chair. She shook with rage. "You warmonger, are our allies aware of what you intend to do?"

"If they've been paying attention," said Trump, refusing to look at her, obviously wishing he could fire her as well.

"You're planning to nuke Iran, aren't you? You've fallen in with Ted and his alt-right millenarian madness, haven't you?"

Trump smirked. "Ted is many things, many terrible things. But he's way past millennial, let me tell you."

Cruz smiled. "Donald, you couldn't tell a millenarian from a millennial, could you?"

"And I could care less," said Trump.

"Couldn't," said Carson. "You *couldn't* care less."

"That's right," said Trump. "Alright, let's push Wild Eyes over the edge. Henry," he turned to leveraged buy-out guru and Treasury Secretary Henry Kravis. "How are we doing?"

"Too soon to tell."

Trump arched an eyebrow. "Did Sarah pay you to keep it short?" He got a chuckle from everyone but Kravis. "So Yellen's fine going negative?"

"Desperate times," said Kravis. "She's just not convinced it's going to work. And now she's afraid she's out of bullets." Kravis's lips bent into a smile. "Of course it's not much of a bullet if it doesn't even penetrate the skin."

"People, and banks," said Trump, "they are going to have so much cash, they are going to have to put it to good use. Starting businesses, lending, spending."

Kravis stared at him. "We'll see. I've had a few legislators approach me about doing a deal on taxes."

"I figured killing the income tax might get them to the table," said Trump. "Too late though."

"We could use some revenue," said Kravis.

Trump had retreated into his thoughts. "You know it's not fair," he said. "People love what I'm doing. But they're so afraid Hillary is going to change everything when she takes over."

Eyes went to Warren, who only smiled.

DEPLOYED IN

THE DESERT

ON WEDNESDAY MARCH 15TH, TRUMP visited 2 towns along the broad Iraq-Syrian front, or what the Muslim world was calling the Christian Crusade. The US Army was engaging Iranian proxies much more often than the Islamic State. The result was that US forces were now on the doorsteps of Baghdad and Aleppo.

"People ask me," Trump said at a press conference in front of an executive officer tent flapping in the desert wind. "They ask Secretary of State Petraeus and Defense Secretary Bolton, are we going into Baghdad? Are we going into Aleppo? Will we continue on into Damascus? I tell them, we'll see. It depends. Probably. Probably. Are we going to Tehran? Nobody has asked me that. Maybe they should. We'll see.

"I don't like what the mullahs, the Ayatollah, the Iranian leaders are doing, I'll tell you that. It's not good. We've lost some great men and women in these battles—not nearly as many people as the enemy has lost, believe me. Not even a comparison. But we've lost our people, and I'm terribly sad about that.

"We're prepared to pay that price. I can tell you I've heard that message over and over, from every general and every soldier I talk to. What is happening here is a direct threat to the security of the United States, and the world. We won't leave until that threat is eliminated. Completely.

"What about Israel? I'm asked about that. Israel has their own issues. Israel can take care of themselves. If Israel is attacked, we'll do whatever it takes to help them. Israel is a great ally of the United States. But what we're doing here has nothing to do with them. Nothing to do with the Palestinians. They have to figure that out."

He opened the floor to questions. A *New York Times* reporter went first.

"It appears the Islamic State is retreating to Dabiq for their last stand. What are your thoughts?"

"They won't be a problem much longer."

"Can you elaborate?"

"No. You'll see."

"You mentioned Baghdad, Aleppo and Damascus," said a CBS reporter. "Will you invade them?"

"It depends," said Trump. "It depends like I said on Iran. All these cities, these governments, they're basically puppets of the Ayatollah, okay? So if we think it's necessary to end the puppet show, the threat, then we'll do whatever it takes. We aren't going anywhere for a long time, okay? And these countries, these governments are paying for our invasion with their oil."

"Some people are saying," said a BBC reporter, "that you are intentionally pushing up the price of oil to support Vladimir Putin in Russia. How do you respond?"

"That's stupid. That's a stupid question, okay? Oil has nothing to do with anything. Of course we're disrupting the market. But remember it helps our oil producers, too. Higher prices are good for them. What's the price right now? $80? That's not a bad price. I hope it doesn't get any higher."

"Many people," said a reporter from the French paper *Le Monde*, "are concerned that the US actions here will push the world economy into a recession, or worse. Do you see that happening?"

"The world economy is already failing miserably—" Trump jumped at the sound of artillery some miles in the distance. "That was close. I can't predict the world economy, okay? There are a lot of variables going on there. I'll say I'm not happy with the US economy. If we hadn't done what we've done, with taxes and immigration and everything else we've accomplished, let me tell you, it would be worse. Much worse.

"But it's not good. There are no jobs, okay? Not enough jobs. Everybody's wondering what's coming next.

"The worst thing is uncertainty. That's what this 6-month presidency creates. Everyone is afraid: 'What's the next president going to do?' Hillary, okay? They're afraid of her. So we're going to do what we can to take away that uncertainty."

Every hand went up and everyone shouted questions. Trump gazed upon them with disdain and then called on an MSNBC reporter.

"Can you elaborate on what you're doing to take away the uncertainty

of a Clinton presidency?"
  Trump smiled. "Soon. Soon."

THE OFFER

BILL CLINTON CONTINUES TO ATTEND secret meetings that a prudent man might not. It's why a lot of people are looking forward to Hillary's presidency. I had the pleasure of sitting in on the latest example.

"Bill," said Trump. "Glad you could come."

"I'm a sucker for an intriguing invitation," said Bill. He was so affable, I couldn't tell whether he was poking fun at himself. "You've had quite the eventful first couple months. How are you holding up?"

"Great," said Trump. He had them facing each other in low-backed chairs, a low table partially separating them. "We've made good progress. I'm only hoping it will continue after my first term."

Bill chuckled. "If you're looking for insight on that, you're talking to the wrong Clinton. For better or worse, I'm going to have next-to-no say during Hillary's presidency."

"What are you going to do?"

"Well…" Bill wore a disappointed, wry smile. "There won't be much in the way of Clinton Foundation work for me. I'll have to find a new cause."

"I'd like to offer you the greatest cause on earth," said Trump. "A life-long position. Once in a lifetime."

"Head librarian at the Trump presidential library?"

Trump soured. "It's going to be twice as big as yours, that's all I know. But what I'm talking about is the Supreme Court."

Clinton opened his mouth but nothing came out. He closed it and cocked his head. Twice he started to reply and changed his mind. Then, "Are you pulling my leg?"

"Never," said Trump.

Clinton's eyes went to me and I'm glad this was news to me too because he would have read me like a book. "You're trying to interfere with Hillary's presidency," he said to Trump.

"I don't want her to be president."

Bill's mouth stayed open, stunned. "The Supreme Court. That's a helluva bribe."

Trump shook his head. "It's no bribe. You know how I think of you. You'd be great. No one finds common ground like you. No one sells it like you. You'd be the de facto chief justice."

Clinton sat back, marveling. "Supreme Court, huh?"

"First president ever. Right?" he asked me like I was the resident historian.

"I think so."

Bill nodded to me. "How's this guy treating you?"

"Really, really great," I said.

"You'd be deciding the most important questions in the world," said Trump. "That would be quite a legacy."

Bill cocked his head, perhaps picturing it. "Yeah."

Trump stood. "Bill, we go back a long way. Our relationship is bigger than what's going on with Hillary. Say okay, say yes."

Bill stood and they shook hands. "The answer will have to be 'no,' I suppose…but…" He nodded to me and left the suite.

"I have to head over to the White House for a Medal of Honor ceremony," Trump said to me. "Let's get a sandwich."

Two assumptions I had about Trump have been proven wrong. The first was the most recently formed, when I realized how much time we were going to spend together, and how open Trump is to letting me listen to practically everything he says and hears. I assumed we would grow quite close.

But not at all. We haven't shared a smile or an inside joke. I haven't seen him with his guard down, all human and vulnerable and revealed. I don't think Trump has a guard; he doesn't seem to have a private side to protect. He never seems to have the need to let his hair down.

I realize that's a particularly vivid metaphor for Donald Trump; but I think it's perfect. That hair has no ability or desire to come down.

We did indeed get a sandwich together from the hotel's special Trump commissary. And we ate it together in the limo on the way to the White House. Trump was on the phone chewing in the ear of one of his property managers who seemed to have received conflicting instructions from Trump and his son Eric.

"Alright, whatever he wants," said Trump. "Tell him what I think, then let him decide. Let me know which way you go."

I listened. That's what he paid me to do, listen and choose what to pass along. He put no restrictions on my access or my choices. It went without saying he would fire me if he didn't like what I conveyed to "my community."

At the White House he stopped briefly to say hello to Ivanka and Don Jr. They conducted business, Trump business, personal business, maybe monkey business. Trump didn't consult with them, and as the limo call testified, neither did they seek his counsel. Contrary to my other false assumption, this was not a tight, insular family.

His kids (and wife) had probably long ago given up trying to manage him. After awarding the Medal of Honor posthumously to a Marine killed in the current Middle East warfare, Trump used the Rose Garden ceremony to attack Hillary.

"I don't see how she can truly be president. I don't see it, okay? She's crooked. Just look at her family's ongoing dealings with their corrupt foundation. Hillary and Chelsea keep raking in the donations. And the line of donors expecting quid pro quo keeps growing. They're waiting for me to hand the keys over to Hillary. Then everyone's gonna cash in. It's going to be terrible like we've never seen."

A reporter in the back raised his hand. "Hillary has compared her Foundation work to the fact that you and your family haven't relinquished control of the Trump businesses."

"Because they're *businesses*, okay? I wouldn't expect you to understand the difference. But the people do."

"And that is?"

"A business earns revenue, okay? Hillary's crooked foundation solicits donations. Big difference. The people who do business with me? If I don't perform, they lose their money. The donors who give to Hillary? They don't care what the Clintons do with the money. All they care about is access. Pay for play. Have you heard of that? Okay."

"Hillary says—"

"*Risk*. That's the difference. People who do business with me, they don't want favors. They want to make *money*. And if my deal goes bad, and my company goes bankrupt—which Hillary loves to point out, by the way—'oh Trump is so terrible, he files for bankruptcy and loses these people their money.' That's right. Some do lose their money. And they know it can happen in real estate. It happens all the time. All the time.

"But no one loses their money when they slip it into Hillary's pocket. There's no risk being in Hillary's pocket. They'll get the favors they paid for. Believe me."

Another reporter yelled out a follow-up question. It had become a bit of a free-for-all. "So you don't think Hillary is fit to be president? You don't think the 6-month arrangement should be fulfilled?"

Trump thought for a bit. "I don't. I don't think it's going to work. Here's why. I wasn't going to mention this yet. But I think Hillary is going to have a conflict of interest. Today I decided to fill the open seat on the Supreme Court. I offered the job to Bill Clinton."

The assembled gasped, from the reporters to the parents of the Medal of Honor Marine to Secretary of Defense John Bolton.

A CNN reporter found her voice. "You *offered* him the seat?"

"He'll be confirmed 100% by the Senate." Trump snapped his fingers. "Like that. Don't worry. If he wants it, and I hope he does, it's his."

Thirty minutes later Hillary Clinton gave a statement.

"Well," she said with a laugh she seemingly shared with the press and America, "Donald is up to his old shady tricks. Anybody who knows him knew he wasn't going to abide by the Constitution or the arrangement struck by the 9-person Special Presidential Election Commission, comprised of esteemed members of *both* parties I should remind everyone.

"But today's move really stooped to a new, sleazy, cynical low, didn't it? Would Bill make a great justice on the Court? Yes of course. But the nomination has been made as blackmail. Or a bribe, take your pick. It's despicable. And of course the answer is no.

"I'm not in a position—yet—to initiate an investigation of the intent behind this blatant ethical violation. But I strongly urge Congress and *both* parties to do so promptly.

"To this point I've been mostly quiet while this administration has done everything in its power to undermine our Constitution, place our soldiers in harm's way, appease our adversaries and jeopardize freedom in Europe. Freedom that so many of our young men gave their lives for years ago.

"But I can no longer hold my tongue. Donald, you must stop your reckless, unilateral, and probably illegal actions before it's too late. I would say that July 4th can't come soon enough; but that's over 3 months away and I'm afraid it might be too late.

"Short of reconvening the Special Presidential Election Commission to reevaluate its decision, I ask Congress and the American people to be vigilant and to do everything in your power to ensure our Constitution, our servicewomen and servicemen, and our freedoms are protected from the depredations of this administration."

Hillary took no questions.

Trump didn't back down. He doubled down.

HEALING THE SICK

TAX DAY, APRIL 17TH, CAME and Americans filed what could be their last federal income tax return. Our pockets bulged with fatter take-home checks. Those of us with jobs, that is.

The economy continued to tank. For the 5th month in a row, businesses employed fewer people than the month before. The unemployment rate hit 12%. Government tax receipts plunged, military spending skyrocketed and the annual deficit climbed above a trillion.

There was one mixed signal. Wages rose in the first quarter of the year, tugging inflation up with them. Economists saw it as a leading indicator of the impacts from reduced immigration and fines on products from China and US companies manufacturing outside the US.

Trump saw nothing but gloom and blamed it on Hillary. "We have a crisis," he told America in a prime time address. "The moves I've made to help this country and create jobs have been ruined by the threat of a Hillary Clinton presidency. Businesses have money but they're not hiring. People have money but they're not spending.

"This is because everyone knows that as soon as Hillary takes office, she's going to kill everything we've done. She's going to try to drag us back to the failed policies of Barack Obama. Disaster. That will be a complete disaster.

"And everyone knows it. That's why businesses don't dare hire more. They know Hillary is going to tax them and regulate them and open our borders so they can hire cheap illegals who will vote for Democrats. It's terrible I know. But it's true.

"But I'm not standing still. I think Hillary should be ruled ineligible for the presidency, for a lot of reasons. I hope the Election Commission does something. In the meantime I'm going to do 2 things to help make us great again.

"First. This one comes from Ivanka. It comes from the new generation and it's for the new generation. I am a big fan of young people, and I know they feel the same way. Because they know I'm on their side. We have all these colleges charging incredibly high tuition to give our young people degrees they can't use. They pay big, big money for a degree, and then it doesn't get them a job.

"Barack Obama worked really hard to put for-profit schools out of business for this very same thing. That was a disaster for a lot of people, a lot of students who lost their schools, right in the middle of their degree programs. Now we're going to actually do it *right* with our state-run colleges and universities. We're not going to put them out of business; they do some good. But they are going to refund the money to these young people.

"If you have a degree and you've been searching for more than 6 months, and you can't find a job, you're going to get a refund. Half of your tuition.

"These schools can afford it, believe me. They have huge endowments. Most people have no idea. We're going to give them the chance to make these refunds voluntarily. If that doesn't work, we'll withhold any federal payments going to these schools, and give them to their former students instead. If that's still not enough, we'll sue them on these students' behalf. If I were these schools, I wouldn't let it come to that, it might end with them suffering the same fate as the for-profit schools the Obama administration put out of business.

"Next. I've talked to major CEOs of our biggest companies, and they tell me healthcare costs are a problem. So this is long overdue. It's been a busy 3 months, what can I say. I've been very busy. But now it's time to end Obamacare. I hear this from business people. They can't afford to hire people, because healthcare is too expensive.

"Obamacare is a disaster. No insurance company will cover anyone. They can't, it's a loser. The government makes them pay for everything, and they're getting stuck with the sickest people. That's wrong.

"So effective immediately Obamacare is over. 'Oh no,' everybody is screaming. 'Trump's taking us back to the old broken system.' No. That was the old Republican party. They refuse to think there might be a better way.

"But there is a better way and it's called competition. *Competition*. Let me ask you this: Why does everyone have to have car insurance? Because it's the only way the insurance market works. Because it's smart. No one has trouble with car insurance, right? Because it's done right.

"From now on, everybody—*everybody* has to have health insurance. If you can't afford to pay the full amount of the premium, we're going to help. We're going to expand Medicaid. No one is going to be left dying on the street like they are now.

"And to ensure we have real competition, we're going to let insurance companies sell their policies anywhere, any state, the same policies. The states no longer get to tell insurance companies what their policies need to look like, what they need to cover, in great, great detail. We're ending that. It's crazy. That's very expensive for insurance companies, trying to sell and manage 50 different policies.

"And because now they're covering healthy people too, not just the sick people, their costs will come down even further. These changes are going to save insurance companies a *lot* of money. Which means they can lower your premiums. They'll have to. Why? Because another insurance company will. They'll *compete*. Premiums are going to come *down*, and costs are going to come *down*.

"I know the government has hired a lot of people to run Obamacare. So many people, who really aren't helping. The good news is, the insurance companies will be hiring, because they're going to be trying hard for your business. Maybe they'll want to hire the government Obamacare people. We'll see.

"Congress isn't going to like this. They're going to cry that I should have asked them first. But then of course we all know nothing would get done. Congress would get a lot of lunches and dinners and trips and 'political' contributions from lobbyists, lobbyists from the insurance companies and the doctors and the unions and the government—don't forget the government, they're big political spenders, let me tell you.

"Congress would have taken all this money and done nothing. Or worse. I've tried to work with them, both sides. They're not interested in getting things done. They want to get lobbied, they want to get bought. First and foremost, they want to get reelected.

"With all the lobbying that would have happened, they would have come up with something worse than Obamacare.

"They say a good compromise means everyone's unhappy. That's stupid. That's a bad deal, okay? What we're doing here, this is a good deal."

INACTION

FIVE DAYS LATER, APRIL 22ND, the 9 Presidential Election Commissioners were guests on *Dateline*. They were there to discuss the Trump presidency.

"Well I guess when people say it's time for a 3rd political party," said Speaker of the House Ryan, "this is what they're talking about. From any perspective, you would have to say this presidency has been a disaster. Democrat or Republican, hawk or dove, socialist or capitalist, nativist or internationalist…Donald Trump has been a failure.

"The unconstitutional, unilateral actions should shock and appall everyone. Our system of checks and balances are thrown right out the window if Trump is successful."

The interviewer Lester Holt was puzzled. "You say if? Hasn't he been successful?"

Ryan was grim. "To date. There are multiple challenges before the courts."

"Two of his initiatives have already been upheld by the courts though," said Holt. "His Muslim ban and his income tax repeal."

"Therein lies another problem," said Chief Justice Roberts. "Both of those federal court rulings have been challenged before the Supreme Court. In both instances we've split 4-4, albeit with very different bed partners if you will. It's time President Trump uphold the duty of his office and appoint a 9th justice."

"Will someone bring a lawsuit if he doesn't?" said Holt.

The camera panned across 9 cloudy faces.

"Changing the subject slightly," said Holt. "How goes the deliberations on revisions to our presidential election system?"

The camera panned across 9 tight faces. "Our deadline is October 15th," said Justice Roberts. "We'll meet that deadline."

Donald, Melania and Ivanka visited the east end of Minneapolis. With the Minneapolis mayor and Minnesota governor they talked to local reporters against a backdrop of the ruined stadium and deserted office towers, blocks in the distance.

"The mayor and the governor are assuring everyone that the buildings in the impacted zone will be repaired and clean of radiation by Christmas," said a local television reporter. "But we talk to the Vikings and Wells Fargo, the 2 major impacted tenants, and they say they have no plans to return. What should be done?"

Trump shrugged. "We're here to show our support."

"Do you feel it's safe to walk in those buildings? Would Trump buy them as a developer?"

He shrugged again. "We'll see. FEMA is working with local officials and the CDC, the experts. Hopefully when they give the green light, people will feel safe."

"Downtown Minneapolis has been significantly impacted," said a *Star Tribune* reporter. "The local economy is extremely depressed, almost 3 times what we're seeing nationally. We know the national terrorism insurance program is chipping in for the insured losses. What else is the federal government doing to help downtown Minneapolis businesses and the Minnesota economy in general?"

"We stand ready to help," said Trump.

"Our hearts go out to the people of Minnesota," said Melania.

"I'm here to talk about that with the governor and the mayor," said Trump. "We'll work with Congress to get help here."

"With all due respect," said a reporter for the indie paper *City Pages*, "you've never waited for Congress before. Why now?"

Trump jutted out his jaw. "I'll do what I can."

"When will you nominate a Supreme Court justice?" asked the *City Pages* reporter.

This was a topic Trump embraced. "Everybody wants me to appoint a justice. I'm not unhappy with the current situation, to tell you the truth. Republicans are pressuring me, night and day. Immense pressure. They're afraid of what I'm doing, and they're afraid of who Hillary Clinton would appoint."

"Aren't you?"

Trump's lip curled up. "I'm sure I would disagree with whoever she named. But I have to ask you, and I'll ask her: is this so bad? Why do we want one person deciding the law of the land? That's the only time a 9th justice is important, when there's a deadlock. Which is all the time. And then it becomes a political decision. Should the Court be political? I don't think so."

"And if the Supreme Court is deadlocked," the reporter seemed to be thinking rather than reporting, "then the various lower court rulings will stand."

"My father's onto something, isn't he?" said Ivanka. "We'll see if Hillary is that brave."

DECELERATION

THE CABINET MET ON MAY 25th to consider the state of the nation. "What's the latest on ISIS?" said Trump.

Secretary of State Petraeus deferred to Defense Secretary Bolton. "As we expected, they've largely consolidated their forces, such as they are, in Dabiq. Because they've lost so much territory, they've lost a lot of legitimacy in the extremist Muslim community. Their claim to the caliphate depends on holding territory. We've ruined that for them. So they've had relatively few foreign fighters joining them."

"So our work is done," said Vice President Warren.

"If we leave before finishing them," said Petraeus, "they'll just start rebuilding their caliphate. That region is a power vacuum."

"They won't surrender," said Bolton. "They want to fight. They don't have trouble being martyrs. However, we have our hands full with Iran."

"Their support has become much more overt," said JCS chairman Dunford. "We're seeing the Revolutionary Guard fighting side by side with Hezbollah and the Shiite forces in Iraq. Some of which are guerrillas, some regular Iraqi army. To a great extent we're currently at war with Iran."

"They've restarted their nuclear program," said Petraeus. "If it was ever paused, that is. Our allies aren't going to join us in re-imposing sanctions. The Iranians are claiming self-defense, and everyone but Britain is buying it."

"Not to mention the fact that you unilaterally destroyed our agreement with them," said Warren.

"They weren't following it," said Trump.

"You don't know that," said Warren.

"That agreement emboldened the mullahs," said Bolton. "They wouldn't have had the spine, international support or resources to restart their nuclear program if the sanctions had never been lifted."

"Bull," said Warren.

"That agreement has forced us into a corner," said Bolton. "Sanctions are off the table. War is now likely the only way we can prevent them from becoming a rogue nuclear power."

"I was so afraid of seeing you in this chair," Warren said to Bolton. "This is why."

"Okay," said Trump. "How about Israel?"

"They're fully mobilized," said Petraeus. "Lots of activity on the Lebanon border and the Golan Heights. They're worried but ready."

Trump sat deep in his chair with his chin on his chest.

"What are you going to do?" Warren challenged.

"We'll have a plan," said Trump "We have a plan."

Warren snorted.

"Same sunny news on the economy," said Treasury Secretary Kravis. "We're not expecting a positive May jobs report. Rates are remaining below zero, which is of course by design. Everyone is hoarding cash. They're afraid of the stock market, they're unwilling to accept negative investment rates, they're not confident enough in the future to hire or expand or start a business. Because tax receipts have plummeted, the government is running out of money."

"Great," said Trump.

"There are 2 bright spots," said Kravis. "Inner city unemployment rates are actually dropping. Without the illegal immigrant competition, service industries are hiring citizens. And it's pushing up the average wage."

"We're also seeing signs of a drop in the crime rate," said Attorney General Cruz. "Preliminary of course, but encouraging. In the past month we've also refused 3 different requests for a Justice department investigation into local policing. We're forcing the locals to deal with it."

"That's unconscionable," said Warren. "The next shooting of an unarmed black man will be on your hands."

"Elizabeth, no it won't. It will be on the hands of the officer if he's found to be in the wrong. Otherwise—"

"That's the issue," said Warren. "Local jurisdictions will never find the officer to be in the wrong. Look at Baltimore."

"One of the cities demanding federal government intervention was Seattle," said Cruz. "Are you telling me they're a bunch of reactionary racists running Seattle? Or that the citizens aren't capable of turning them out?"

"Racial change in America has only happened with federal intervention," said Warren.

"That's not true," said Cruz.

"I've had enough of this for one day," said Trump. He rose. "Let me know if I need to tell the American people anything."

"The wall is coming along nicely," said Homeland Secretary Rudy Giuliani.

"Great," said Trump as he left the room.

"I think I'm leaving things in good shape."

This Donald Trump said to me as we sat in his Lafayette study. I was drinking a beer, Trump a club soda with lime.

"Really great shape," he said. "For 6 months of work."

"You still have a month left," I said. It was June 4th, with Hillary due to take the reins on Independence Day.

He shook his head. "One month isn't enough time to do anything. Hillary is just going to cast everything I've done as a mistake." He was melancholy like I'd never seen.

I debated how to answer. "She's inheriting a lot of problems."

"So did I. A *lot*. This country was heading the wrong way on everything. Obama thinks he took over at a tough time." He sipped his drink. "Six months wasn't enough time to fix things."

"You actually did a lot."

"No." He rubbed his forehead. "I never should have agreed to this."

I said nothing.

"My legacy might be ruined."

"Your business empire is still intact." The *Wall Street Journal* had just run a lengthy series on various thriving Trump investments in Russia, and Russia's thriving investments in Trump real estate developments, and the ongoing allegations of corrupt appeasement of Putin's aggressions.

"My kids will be fine," he said. He looked so beaten. "That's not what this was about."

"No…" I straddled the line between affirmation and question.

"I owe this country a lot. So very much. I have so much to offer it. I know I could fix a lot of our problems."

"Really, you did a *lot*."

Trump shook his head. "None of it feels permanent. Some was too much, I went too far. Lots of other places I didn't do enough. And there were no deals. No agreement. That's what's satisfying in life. That's what's missing."

"My favorite was the repeal of the income tax," I told him. "Maybe because that made Congress the angriest."

"I cost them a lot of political contributions with that one."

"That's a big win."

Trump shook his head. "I wasn't in this to win," he said. "I really didn't want to beat anybody. I'm a moderate at heart and I came off as a radical. What I really wanted to do was lead and get everyone behind me." He looked at me. "I didn't do that."

Because he didn't ask it in the form of a question, I didn't answer.

HOLIDAY

AND THAT'S HOW THE 6-MONTH 2017 presidency of Donald J. Trump ended. He met individually, sporadically with his cabinet and held 2 more subdued, lackluster press conferences. He chose not to exploit another batch of Hillary Clinton's hacked emails released by Russia that called into question the political pay-to-play of the Clinton Foundation donors.

And then the July 4th holiday was upon us and Hillary Clinton was sworn in as the 45th President of the United States.

HILLARY

REVERSALS

HILLARY CAME IN LIKE A rock star.

She had an entourage, a staff of loyalists that had grown with each of her positions in the federal government, First Lady to Senator to Secretary of State to President. She received a standing ovation from the career civil servants from the various executive offices, packed into the White House foyer and spilling outside, down the halls and up the stairs.

A microphone had been set up for her. "Well, isn't this wonderful. Familiar, wonderful faces everywhere. Let's hear it from those who were here when I was at State."

Probably ¾ of the crowd cheered.

"Okay. Now how about the folks who were here when I was first lady."

At least half the people whooped it up.

"That is so nice," said Hillary. "I'm looking forward to seeing old friends and making new ones." She looked around. "I heard my predecessor didn't spend much time here."

"None!" someone shouted.

Hillary laughed. "Well, you're going to see a *lot* of me. I'm a big fan of face-to-face interactions. I've sort of lost my taste for email."

Lots of laughs.

"Thank you for taking time out of your busy day to welcome me back. I hope you're excited about the next 6 months—and beyond. We are going to get a lot done. I know you are all here in Washington to make a difference. With all the chaos surrounding the election and the distractions since then, I'm guessing it's been difficult."

This was roundly affirmed.

"Well, now the difficulty is going to be keeping up with everything we want to accomplish! I have been champing at the bit to get going. It might have made me slightly tough to be around." She looked coyly at her closest confidantes, Huma Abedin her Labor Secretary and Cheryl Mills her Chief of Staff.

They both hammed up the stress they had suffered with an impatient Hillary.

"Seriously, we have a lot of work to do. Fortunately, I'd like to think I have some practice picking up the pieces of broken policies and putting them back together." Hillary nodded at the murmurs of recognition. "To do that, I'll need to hear from you, about what's working and what's not. Please don't hesitate to find me or my immediate team and let us know what's on your mind."

Hillary surveyed a crowd that seemed overjoyed at the chance to feel valued again. "I can tell you're eager to get going." She received a swell of enthusiasm. "Then let's do it! And tune in tonight. I think you're going to like what you hear."

There was a crowd in that afternoon's cabinet meeting. Every cabinet official had their plus-one or -two; Hillary had plus-10.

Initially that didn't include her vice president, Sean Hannity. He came late to the West Wing cabinet room, and all the seats at the table were taken.

"Sorry Sean," said Hillary. "Capricia keeps us on time." She referred to her calendar coordinator Capricia Marshall. "Maybe in the future you can ask someone to save you a seat."

"No problem whatsoever," said Hannity. "This isn't the first time I've been denied a seat at the table." He came to stand beside me against the wall. "Looks like you can relate."

I was amazed to be there, period. Two years ago I encouraged the Michigan Republican leadership to drop their support for a black, corrupt Detroit politician, knowing it would mean victory for the underdog, white Democrat. Bill Clinton somehow got wind of it and sent me a thank-you card. I had become a Friend of Bill. Someone in Hillary's inner circle must have been persuaded I was valuable in the same role I performed for Trump. Hillary's team, however, required me to vet everything I planned to report out.

"Can we get started?" said Hillary. "I want everyone here to know what I intend to say tonight." She was giving a televised commencement and state of the Union speech.

Chief of Staff Mills spoke up. "The Cliff Notes version: We're reversing and apologizing for everything Donald Trump did."

"Apologies aren't what America is looking for," said Hannity.

Hillary gave him a withering smile. "Mr. Hannity, unlike Fox News, we run things with decorum and order. Under this Compromise, I have to allow you to be my vice president. But that's it. I don't have to let you speak. So until I call on you, please be quiet."

Hannity raised an apologetic hand. "I expected no better treatment from you. I will be sure to prostrate myself before the queen and kiss your ring before I even think of speaking up."

Hillary largely managed to ignore him. "First of all, Paul will be reinstituting the income tax." She referred to Treasury Secretary Paul Krugman, the professorial economist and columnist. "That's a no-brainer. It's my duty, actually. The tax itself is constitutionally protected, and the rate structure is statutorily determined. The president can't even tweak it, much less eliminate it. Despite what one, single federal court has ruled."

"And of course the reinstatement will need to be retroactive to January first." Krugman sat with arms crossed. "It was clearly a sabotage by Trump to torpedo this administration's ability to manage the economy. I don't doubt that if heaven forbid he could steal the presidency for the remaining 3 years, he would reinstitute the tax."

"We do recognize," said Hillary, "that the tax code is broken. So I'm creating a blue ribbon panel of experts to recommend changes, which we will then take to Congress."

"I'm assuming we're discontinuing the sales tax," said Commerce Secretary Jack Lew, Obama's Treasury Secretary. "Will that be retroactive as well, with refunds?"

"We haven't decided what to do with the sales tax," said Krugman.

"Oh boy," said Hannity—then held up his hands and sucked his lips in, as if they were now sewn shut.

"Switching to the border," said Hillary, unamused. "We're halting construction of the wall. As you know there have been serious allegations of mismanagement and corruption, including contractors with ties to Trump."

"We'll put an end to the fraud and abuse," said Homeland Security Secretary Jake Sullivan, one of Hillary's closest aides. "And in the meantime we'll negotiate a path to citizenship for our undocumented workers who have no criminal record. We'll also of course put an end to Trump's discriminatory immigration policy. Muslim, Christian, Jewish, everyone will undergo the same thorough background vetting."

"Speaking of…" Secretary of Defense Michèle Flournoy paused. Flournoy was a high-ranking Defense official for Obama and head of a national security think tank. "…foreign peoples from the Middle East, we have serious issues with multiple countries and non-state actors, caused by our predecessor. We have overextended ourselves in Iraq and Syria. We have already begun pulling back from both countries."

Secretary of State Bill Burns, former ambassador to Russia and a career State department employee, followed on that. "We are also re-implementing our end of the pact we signed with Iran a year ago."

"Now I have heard it all," said Hannity. "Do you really hate this country so much—"

"Out," said Hillary.

"—that you would guarantee Israel's destruction, just to prove how peaceful you are?" He held up his hands as Hillary's aides converged. "I'm going. I've heard enough." At the door he looked back at me. "If you're not going to follow me, I hope you'll at least report this accurately, to anyone who will listen."

He left the room and Hillary said, "Everyone will hear exactly this tonight. The big difference is, everyone but the extreme alt-right will agree it's the right thing to do."

"We see the Iran agreement," said Secretary of State Burns, "as crucial to deescalating tensions across the Middle East, and allowing us to reinstitute the monitoring system to ensure Iran cannot restart its nuclear program."

"This will also allow us to focus on the task at hand," said Hillary. "While we still don't have definitive proof of the organization behind the dirty bomb, we can be fairly confident it was at least ISIS-inspired. Unlike Trump, and Bush, we aren't going to be distracted from our primary mission of ending ISIS. We're going to destroy them in Dabiq."

Homeland Secretary Sullivan served up a fat softball for Hillary to slug. "The fact that this lines up with their end of times prophecy be damned?"

Hillary wore a steely look. "ISIS prophecy be damned."

"Meanwhile our good friend Vlad Putin seems to be behaving himself," said Burns.

"Just a coincidence?" said Sullivan, still pitching to Hillary.

"Nothing that man does is coincidental," said Hillary with an insider's chuckle. "I'm going to be spending quite a bit of time with the leaders of our European allies. We've neglected them for too long. Smart power theory tells us we need to neutralize Russia's economic extortion with trade support."

"The Europeans aren't willing to get in the trading bed with us if they're going to come away dirty," said Sullivan.

Burns shot the younger man a look that told him to back away from his domain of statecraft.

Sullivan ignored him. "We need to prove the playing field will be level in terms of human rights."

"We're going to set their minds at ease," said Hillary. "I'm going to spend most of my speech tonight talking about the *positive*. Won't that be nice for a change?"

Labor Secretary Huma Abedin cleared her throat, seemingly unnecessarily, her voice eternally soft and pure. "We're introducing a government insurance option to provide some well-needed competition to the bloated private insurers." She went to take a sip of water and paused. "Oh, did I mention, we're tossing out what Trump tried to do. We will retain the enhanced subsidy structure to ensure everyone can afford their premiums. The good news is, with the government now providing a cost-efficient insurance alternative, those subsidies will be much lower than they would have been under Trump."

"We expect most companies, not to mention individuals," said Commerce Secretary Lew, "will choose the federal insurance option. It should put extreme pressure on the insurance companies."

"Not if they finally cut their bloat," said Hillary. "Then they'll be fine."

"Of course that will be when the Greenland glaciers return to normal," said Sullivan.

"I.e.," said Chief of Staff Mills, adding to the rueful chuckling, "when Congress gets a clue or Hell freezes over."

Energy Secretary Ken Salazar spoke for the first time. "It could come sooner than you might think. We're accelerating our Clean Air and Water deadlines, and putting sharp teeth in our penalties. It will mean an accelerated move out of coal and oil, and into alternatives. At the same time we're creating a robust job training and transition program to assist displaced fossil fuel workers."

Sullivan nodded thoughtfully. "That will all help put the Europeans' fears to rest."

Hillary tap-tap-tapped the table. "The Europeans haven't seen anything yet. I guess I wasn't completely forthcoming about my speech tonight. It's going to include a little bit more than what we've discussed here…"

REDIRECTION

DESPITE CAJOLING AND NEAR-PLEADING, HILLARY wouldn't ruin her big reveal. That night from the Oval Office she described everything discussed at the cabinet meeting, and then made the biggest announcement.

"As you all know, this country is suffering through the beginning of what our best economists say could be the worst depression since the 1930s. It has been caused by the turmoil surrounding the last election, and not so coincidentally by the administration charged with the nation's wellbeing these past 6 months.

"We need a serious, significant, historically-tested response. We all know how badly things could have ended if FDR hadn't designed the greatest job creation initiative in world history. And by any measure he probably waited too long.

"We're not going to wait. As the Trump economic crisis unfolded, my team has been working around the clock to create a comprehensive plan to put America back to work. This jobs program isn't a trickle-down giveaway like so many failed, so-called free market initiatives where tax credits are doled out to corporations who are entrusted to do the right thing.

"Instead we will directly employ millions of our hardworking citizens, in our fabulous cities, our beautiful towns, and our bountiful agricultural regions.

"We will rebuild our infrastructure! Our crumbling roads and failing, unsafe bridges. We will significantly upgrade our inadequate, out-of-date information highway—because you can drive all day and still not get the message, unless our data backbone is strong!

"This is the backbone of America! It's frankly ailing. We have too many frayed, missing or decrepit stretches of critical highway, both physical and electronic. It's time we upgraded to the 21st century!"

If there had been a live, partisan audience, they would have been cheering.

"More details will be forthcoming. But know now that if you are unemployed, or under-employed, or working in the shadows at below living wages, help is on the way.

"I'm not setting a quota on the size of this effort; I leave that to you. I leave that to the popular demand, the need for work and the opportunity to make an honorable living serving this country and putting a good meal on your family's table and a roof over their heads."

After the *On Air* light went dark, Hillary got out of the big chair and stood gazing out the window. Bill Clinton breezed in as the television crew filed out.

"I watched on the monitor. You looked great." He pecked her cheek. "I have some folks from the Gates Foundation waiting in the next room. They're looking forward to meeting you."

Hillary growled at him. "It has been a long first day. No."

Bill rolled easily with it. "I'll have Capricia set something up. The Gates folks have some great ideas to leverage this public investment and multiply it with private funds. A lot of companies they work with are eager to get involved in this effort."

Capricia received quiet instructions on dinner from Hillary and left the room, with the Clintons slowly bringing up the rear. "The jobs are going to be direct federal hires," Hillary told Bill.

"This stimulus is going to be big enough," said Bill, "we're going to need some help. Involving Gates and other private philanthropists will create a lot of goodwill for all involved."

"I'm going to name Philippe as special assistant for job works," Hillary named long-time aide Philippe Reines. "Set up the meeting with him."

"They're right in the next room, it would go a long way if you would stop in, real briefly—"

"No, Bill."

CAMPAIGNING

JUST OVER A WEEK INTO Hillary's term, Ruth Bader Ginsburg passed away. Now there were 2 vacancies to be filled on the Supreme Court.

A few days later Hillary reviewed her notes for the speech she was giving that morning at the funeral. I monkeyed with a microphone she would be wearing later in the day at a recognition event I had organized for Jack and Jill of America volunteers and youth leaders. It was a challenge to affix it discretely to her jacket without losing sound quality or her patience.

I retreated across her office to the wireless speaker. "You want to rehearse out loud for me?"

She cleared her throat. That came through loud and clear.

"Ruth was a unique woman," Hillary picked up in the middle of the speech. "She was determined to work within the rules and confines of the system to ensure it protected the interests of the minority against the tyranny of the majority."

I dimmed the speaker and routed her mic to my earbud to better assess the sound quality.

"But she was never afraid to step outside of the system, to voice her opinion on the state of our society as one of our wisest commentators. Sometimes that got Ruth in trouble…"

A knock at the door and a man entered. John Podesta, I would learn, former chief of staff for Bill Clinton and chairman of Hillary's 2016 presidential campaign.

Hillary gave me the skedaddle look. I gathered my equipment and did so.

"What brings you here?" Hillary asked Podesta.

"Opportunity," said Podesta.

I could hear them. In my ear. Hillary still wore the microphone.

"The most optimistic motivational coach couldn't honestly describe what I'm facing as opportunities," said Hillary.

I was wiretapping the President. I hovered in the anteroom, afraid I had already heard more than she would appreciate or tolerate. They continued talking as I stood in limbo.

"I am very sorry about Ruth's passing," said Podesta. "What an amazing woman."

"And opportunity?" Hillary jabbed him.

"Of course. It's time to make lemonade. Your nominations can make Ruth proud."

"You sentimental fool."

Podesta chuckled. "You can also guarantee the country's future. And yours."

"I already know who I'm nominating," said Hillary. "Merrick and Srinivasan."

"Because they're moderate and easy."

"Ha! There is no such thing as easy for me, with Republicans or Democrats. As you well know."

"Right," said Podesta. "You nominate two judges who Republicans can find no fault with, who come from Republican-style backgrounds, and you are still going to be blocked and harassed every step of the way by the Republicans on the Judiciary committee. And meanwhile your Democratic allies will scream that you've abandoned them."

"What's new," said Hillary. "I'm accustomed to lose-lose. But at least we'll eventually get it done."

"*You'll* be done," said Podesta. "The progressive element in our party will never forgive you. They'll abandon you in the reelection. Trump will win."

There was no going back for me now. I settled into a chair and pretended to work on my laptop.

"So what's your plan, John?"

"Go big. Re-nominate Merrick Garland, sure. But go big on the other one. Amy Klobuchar."

"And when the filibustering begins, and never ends?" said Hillary. "I'm not into hollow, moral losses."

"No filibuster. You make a deal with the key Judiciary Republicans before you announce the nominations. Make them part of a package deal."

There was a pause. "They pick up an early shot at Amy's Senate seat," said Hillary, warming to the idea.

"Mm-hm," said Podesta.

"Merrick's a moderate, which frankly is the best they can expect on Scalia's replacement. And with Amy taking Ruth's seat, we're replacing like with like."

"Yep," said Podesta. "But it's going to take more."

"I don't want to give them *anything*," said Hillary. "They don't deserve anything more."

"Hil," said Podesta, "this is once in a lifetime. Getting Amy in would be epochal. It would nearly guarantee the right decision, every decision, for the next 20 years."

"I agree. But we have them over a barrel."

"And they'll pull us right over with them, if they can. You're right, they lost. Their man—if we can call Trump that—failed to take advantage of the opportunity. He failed to fulfill his *duty*, to nominate someone. The American public, everyone except the rabid Republicans, will be behind you. But that doesn't mean we can get them out of committee."

"I'm going to be late for the funeral." Hillary was frustrated. "What do you suggest, John?"

"What's their next biggest fear for the Court?"

"Breyer retiring."

"So guarantee them Srinivasan next."

"Okay…"

"That's probably still not quite enough," said Podesta. "If it was me, I'd also give them guns. Promise to go silent, no legislation."

"Good God," said Hillary. She sighed. "Anything else?"

"Maybe pot too."

There was a tap on my shoulder. Hillary's calendar coordinator Capricia stood over me.

"Are you deaf?" she said.

"Make this work," Podesta said in my ear, "and you're gold for the next 7 years."

"Really focused," I said to Capricia, "polishing my introduction for this afternoon's—"

"This isn't a public workspace."

"Sorry." I slapped the laptop shut and swept up the speaker and made for the door. "Oh, tell Hillary I need to pick up the microphone before she heads over to the funeral, okay?"

DIRTY FINGERPRINTS

THE PULLBACK FROM BAGHDAD AND Aleppo was largely complete by August 1st when Hillary and 15 of her closest aides received an update from Defense chief Flournoy, Secretary of State Burns and Joint Chiefs Chairman Dunford, retained from the Trump administration.

"Our primary concern right now is the Russians," said Flournoy. "We've told them we're not interested in a joint operation. Now it seems we're in a race to take credit for finishing off ISIS."

"Why don't we let them?" said Homeland Secretary Sullivan.

Flournoy paused without looking at him and spoke to Hillary. "As you know, tensions are extremely high. We're right on the Turkish border. We don't need a Putin-Erdogan moment. And both the Turks and the Saudis see the Russians facilitating the Iran-Syria axis, potentially creating an Iran-to-Lebanon Shiite corridor."

"In general," said Burns, "we don't want the Russians asserting themselves as the dominant superpower in the Middle East."

"Or do we?" said Sullivan. With a raised finger he cut off Burns and Flournoy's objections. "Don't worry, we aren't going to let the Russkies become a dominant regional player. But we and Europe have a lot to gain if Putin spreads himself too thin."

"We don't want to operate in the same theater with Russia," said Burns. "And we don't cede control of the Middle East to Putin. Thin or not."

Hillary shifted in her chair. Everyone was attuned to her, turning to listen and waiting for her to speak. "Nobody, not us, not Russia, is going to control the Middle East. Maybe Russia should take their turn zoo-keeping the animals."

"Hillary," said Burns, "we can't desert our allies."

"We'll be ready to respond to any threat to Israel," said Hillary. "We're not reducing our defensive posture or footprint."

"So we let Russia continue to bomb Assad's enemies in Syria?" Burns' voice rose. "What if they decide to help clear the Kurds from Iraq, too?"

"Come on, Burnsie," said Sullivan. "That's not going to happen."

Burns stared at him. "It's such a disappointment when the product falls so short of the packaging."

A young man slipped into the room, mouthed an apology to Hillary and whispered in Sullivan's reddened ear.

"Oh shit," said Sullivan. He waved his assistant out and took a deep breath before announcing to the room, "We have a positive ID on the Minneapolis dirty bomb. Iran's fingerprints are all over it."

IRAN:

IN DRIVER'S SEAT OR

CROSSHAIRS

THE REVELATION HIT THE NEWS 5 days later, Monday August 7th. Hillary's team convinced the press to stay silent while the US prepared and then launched a devastating bombing run on 2 of Iran's less–protected nuclear facilities.

Iran responded by bombing Sunni adversaries, hitting Riyadh, Saudi Arabia and Dubai in the United Arab Emirates. They threatened to close the Strait of Hormuz to oil tankers.

Russia offered to play a peacekeeping role and mediate discussions in Moscow. Meanwhile Syria unleashed a fresh, Russian-backed offensive against rebel-held and rebel-sympathetic towns, unleashing a fresh wave of refugees that overwhelmed the camps established by Turkey in northern Syria, piling up on the Turkish border and sweeping into the Mediterranean, precariously en route for Greece and Europe.

"We have a helluva problem," said Secretary of State Burns, with his predecessor David Petraeus sitting across from Hillary and Defense Secretary Flournoy as Air Force One flew to Ramstein Air Base in Germany. "Congress is debating today whether to declare war on Iran. The odds are good."

"Well, ultimately they don't get to decide," said Hillary.

"Just so you know, polls are for it," said Chief of Staff Mills.

"I don't care about that either," said Hillary.

"One way or the other," said Burns, "we can't let Congress lead."

"Which is why we're meeting with our allies today," said Homeland

Secretary Sullivan.

"Same issue," said Burns, "same response. We can't defer to our allies or let them lead."

"I'd say we already claimed the leadership role," said Sullivan. "We're bombing the shit out of Iran."

"An objective observer would term it largely symbolic," said Burns. "We haven't hit the hardened sites where the real nuclear work takes place. And we're not undertaking a large-scale troop mobilization suggesting much more to come."

"We're just getting going bombing," said Hillary. "Michèle has a campaign ready to go."

"And assuming this trip goes well," said Sullivan, "we'll have our allies on board to join in. Largely symbolic of course," he said sarcastically.

"So we're willing to put boots on the ground in Syria to destroy the ISIS terrorists," said Burns, "but we won't do the same for the Iranian terrorists?"

"I didn't put those boots in Syria," said Hillary. "I was just left to finish the job."

"Same situation, but vastly different players," said Sullivan. "That calls for a different response."

Petraeus, now Hillary's special envoy to the Middle East, finally spoke. "We need to identify our preferred end result in order to determine our approach."

It was obvious Burns understood Petraeus was interviewing for his job. "We're already in agreement on the necessary ending."

"I'm not sure that's true," said Hillary.

"Ending Iran's state-sponsored terrorism," said Burns, sounding extremely frustrated. He moved on to debating the approach. "Bombing them will only harden Khamenei's resolve."

Sullivan chuckled. "Burnsie has all the answers. All that's left for us is but to serve."

Hillary regarded Sullivan dourly but backed him. "You assume something that's not settled wisdom, Bill. I think the key here is nuclear proliferation. There will always be terrorism, whether it's state-sponsored, non-state sponsored, or lone wolves. To pretend terrorism ends with an invasion of Iran is naïve."

"'Invade Iran,'" said Sullivan. "I get ill just hearing that term. And so do our allies."

Hillary continued. "Nuclear weapons is another issue. By inflicting significant damage with the goal of eliminating the nuclear capability in Iran, we can send a strong message to the mullahs as well as North Korea and Pakistan."

"Christ," Burns erupted, standing. "This isn't about nuclear proliferation! They ruined a large piece of one of our major cities. They attacked our homeland! Isn't that your responsibility, Jake? Protecting the homeland?"

Sullivan became extra cool as Burns lost his. "I don't know about you, Bill, but to me the responsibility of protecting our people also includes not sending our young men and women to die in droves in a desert halfway around the globe."

Burns jabbed his finger at the floor. "Sometimes that's what it takes to defend the country and our kids' future."

"The Iranians claim they didn't know this nuclear material had left the country," said Sullivan. "And that they had no knowledge this group was going to attack."

Burns wasn't having it. "Whether or not they gave the final green light, they trained, equipped, armed and targeted these guys. Don't waste our time with that kind of naiveté."

"I'm telling you how the international community is going to see it," said Sullivan. "We won't have their backing."

Hillary looked up at Burns. "I'm not invading alone and leaving with a Bush-Iraq legacy, I'll tell you that."

Burns seethed, shaking his head. "Libya really ended it for you, didn't it?"

Hillary glared. "You're out of line, Bill."

Burns turned to Petraeus. "Are you just going to sit there like a bump on a log? I know you have an opinion."

Petraeus nodded. "I believe the boss has made up her mind. Now it's time to get behind it."

Hillary might as well have stood up and shook Petraeus's hand and congratulated him on winning the job.

Mills turned to me and said, "Nothing leaves this plane." Friend of Bill I might be, but Mills and Hillary's power circle weren't enamored with me or my presence.

When we landed, Burns submitted his resignation and flew home commercial. Hillary named Petraeus to succeed him as Secretary of State. The Senate convened promptly to confirm him.

SEPARATION OF POWERS

IN PARIS THE US RECEIVED limited commitments of support from France, Britain and Australia. The UN Security Council deadlocked on force, preferring to explore a resumption of sanctions, pending a full investigation into Iran's ties to the US dirty bombing.

Israel provided a public full-throated approval of bombing, while behind the scenes they argued for a ground invasion to topple the mullahs. Saudi Arabia and Jordan provided clearance for the Israelis to fly missions through their airspace.

However, the Israeli air force's contributions were relatively limited due to the distance involved and the heavy payloads required to damage Iran's more well-protected nuclear sites. The Saudis did not grant basing permission, forcing the US to accommodate the Israeli operations at our various regional bases.

It was left to the massive US bunker-busting armaments to attempt to destroy Iran's deep-mountain hardened sites at Fordow and Natanz.

"Without eyes on the ground," said Flournoy in a private White House dining room on September 5th, "we're not going to be able to confirm complete destruction. Nor whether we haven't missed any secret sites."

Speaker of the House Paul Ryan buttered his bread. "You have Congress's authorization for those eyes. We declared war. What's the hold-up?"

Hillary smiled. "There's no hold-up. We're not going in with troops."

"There's absolutely no way we're satisfied—"

"Paul," Hillary cut him off. "We didn't set up this courtesy meeting to debate. We're telling you what we're doing so you can bring accurate information back to your chambers."

"We appreciate it," said Senate Majority Leader Dick Durbin. "Of course our role isn't to act as the administration's mouthpiece."

"I was in your shoes," said Hillary. "I understand your role."

"Maybe not *my* shoes," Durbin referenced her junior status in the Senate. "I'm not insulting your intelligence. I am suggesting you could benefit from the perspective of the gentlewoman and gentlemen assembled here."

"I have to say I'm not feeling very gentle these days," said House Minority Leader Nancy Pelosi. "We are catching holy hell from constituents, the press, our families—you should hear the dressing down I received from my grandchildren the other day. Even they recognize that we're handing over the legislative keys to the president."

"Finish that," said Hillary. "You handed the keys to President Trump."

"And Obama," said Senate Minority Leader Mitch McConnell. "And Clinton. And I don't mean Bill."

Hillary laughed. "We're the ones handing the keys back to you."

"We're reversing every unilateral, unconstitutional action by Trump," said Labor Secretary Huma Abedin as she cut her salad with knife and fork. "We're not relying on the courts to do their jobs."

"Putting everything back where unilateral, unconstitutional President Obama had them," said Ryan.

Hillary sipped her tea. "Feel free to pass meaningful legislation any time."

"Believe it or not," said Pelosi, "we're working on it."

"In the meantime," said Abedin, "after a spike in the uninsured under Trump, we've already significantly increased the number of people with health insurance."

"With an illegitimate, so-called 'competing' federal insurance company," said McConnell.

"Which is drastically underpricing the cost of care," Ryan followed.

"That's called savings," said Abedin. "From cutting out the absurd profits Trump handed the insurance industry."

"No one in private industry enjoys absurd profits,' said Ryan. "At least not for long. If there's one thing competition does, it's root out absurd profits. And modest profits. Your side doesn't call it cutthroat competition for nothing."

"We don't gain with an 'us' versus 'them' mentality," said Hillary.

"Let's operate in the real world, Mrs. President," said McConnell. "There are stark and deep philosophical divisions between us."

"I'm actually being historically accurate," Hillary countered. "When it has been 'we,' this country has always found that bridge to common ground."

Ryan swallowed a bite of sole and wiped his lips. "That common ground is going to be a mountain of unsustainable debt. Free tuition," he counted off on his fingers, "free healthcare, and free jobs. But none of that is free. The markets are trying to teach you that lesson."

Interest rates had been moving up since the announcement of the open-ended, federally-funded jobs program. August economic activity showed inflation jumping more than a full percentage point. In 2 months the country had gone from deflation to breaking through the Fed's inflation ceiling. This had spooked the financial markets, driving interest rates skyward.

Treasury Secretary Krugman chewed vegetarian meatloaf as he spoke. "We're on top of it. We were quick to issue our bonds and take advantage of negative rates."

Ryan leaned in. "But not for the long-term timeframes you needed. Instead of having to pay the debt back in 15-20 years, it's going to be less than 5 years. Of course there won't be money in the Treasury to do that—without a massive tax increase."

"We'll be eliminating the massive giveaways to the upper class," said Hillary.

"I won't respond to that other than to say it couldn't be nearly enough," said Ryan. "So you're going to have to refinance the debt by issuing new bonds. And at that point you'll be paying a much, much higher interest rate. A budget buster. You won't be able to euphemize it as an 'investment.'"

"How cynical can you get?" said Krugman. "Since when is an investment in our people and our communities a euphemism?"

Ryan gave him a grim-lipped smile. "You're Santa Claus handing out empty presents, Paul. Inflation is going to erode every bit of spending power in the dollars you're forking over willy-nilly."

"That's called wage growth, Paul," said Krugman. "I know you're only in favor of income that trickles down. But this country is desperate for living wages."

"I remember a little thing called stagflation," said McConnell. "As soon as the government stops printing money, the real economy is going to show its stripes. It won't be pretty."

"Classic Keynesian theory supports everything we're doing," said Krugman. "When the economy gets back to stable footing, we back off on the stimulus."

"Of course it won't work," said Ryan. He pushed away his plate. "And in the meantime you're rewarding contractors who are adept at bellying up to the government trough and destroying other small businesses who can't compete with the inflated wages."

Krugman arched an eyebrow. "When humans drive animals into extinction, capitalists extol the virtues of Darwinian competition. But when it happens to businesses, it's a crime."

Ryan was shocked. "The government isn't supposed to drive its people to extinction."

Krugman spread his hands. "You know as well as I do, Paul. The government *is* the people."

Durbin intervened. "We're running short on time. I know the administration brought us here for their slideshow, but Congress would also like to tell you what we have in mind. As Nancy said, we do have legislation in the works."

"Nothing on sensible background checks for military-style assault weapons," said Pelosi, giving Hillary a less-than-endearing look. "Heaven forbid."

Hillary stared at Pelosi and shook her head, warning her away.

Pelosi dropped it. "We are however writing bills on immigration, fuel standards, minimum wage and tuition funding, among other things."

Hillary gave Ryan and McConnell a wry smile. "Of course none of those attempts to give the American people what they're asking for are going to amount to anything, are they? Republicans aren't interested in governing. They're far too busy conducting frivolous hearings."

"Unfortunately," said McConnell, "every email we pry out of you by subpoena leads us to another dark and likely illegal place. If the Clinton Foundation had put up the firewall like it promised when you were in the Senate and at State, we wouldn't be forced to spend so much time pursuing justice."

"For one thing," said Hillary, "it would be nearly criminal for the Foundation to stop receiving donations. The work we're doing around the world is saving lives. Particularly young women in conservative, repressive societies."

Ryan patted the table. "By all means continue the good work. But then you can't hold political office! You can't mix private donations and government largesse—that's the definition of corruption."

"That sounds like campaign financing to me," said Abedin.

"That's a regulated process," said Ryan.

"Regulated corruption," said Abedin.

"All of this is moot," said Mills, longtime lawyer for Hillary. "There has never been any indication of pay-to-play in any of the donations received by the Foundation."

"Actually there are plenty of indications," said McConnell. "We're confident laws were broken and improper favors were granted. Unfortunately it takes a lot of time to cut through all the obstructions you've thrown up."

"This has been great," said Hillary, rising. "I'll look forward to getting together again next year."

"We're honored to be the first to receive an invite to your retirement party," said McConnell.

"Ha-ha-ha," Hillary laughed, appearing to truly enjoy the sharp back and forth. "We'll probably both die of old age in office, won't we Mitch?"

"Mitch isn't as old as he looks," said Durbin. "The Senate pickles the soul, not the flesh."

McConnell chuckled but his gaze had never left Hillary. "It's time for the nation to heal and come together, Madame President. Like it or not, thanks to the Clinton legacy you are a divisive force. It will be the best thing for the country if you announce that you are stepping aside after this 6-month term."

"So nice of you to provide that advice, Mitch. Is that part of your grand plan to install the great uniter, Donald Trump? Or maybe it's Sean Hannity?"

"Don't worry," said Ryan. "We're having the same conversation with Donald. And I have to tell you, if you agree to do the same, I think he'll go along with it."

INNER CIRCLE

AN INVITE HIT MY CALENDAR for September 26th with Cheryl Mills, Philippe Reines and Capricia Marshall. I have to admit I felt a surge of pride. It's easy to make cynical comments about the cool kids' clique when you're on the outside. And equally difficult to maintain that detached perspective when you're invited in.

We met in Philippe's office of the special assistant for jobs creation. To get there I walked past maybe 10 offices of lesser special assistants all reporting to Philippe, and his 4-person administrative support team in an outer office. Philippe, Cheryl and Capricia were waiting when I arrived. Philippe pointed me to a chair.

"Hey guys, what's up?"

Cheryl laced her fingers around a crossed knee and leaned toward me. "Your time in this administration. Please hand over your security badge, government ID, laptop and iPhone."

I was stunned. "Why?"

"Why?" said Philippe. "Why did it take us so long? Is that your question?"

Oh my God I knew it, they know about my personal Watergate moment! "What in the world are you talking about?"

"I'll ask you once," said Reines as he came around his desk, "and you better not fucking lie to me. Did you know about the deal Hillary made with Grassley and Johnson?"

"Uh…" Yep it made sense Hillary went to Chuck Grassley and Ron Johnson for her Supreme Court nominations. "…not really…" They're both on the Senate Judiciary committee, Grassley as the ranking Republican, while Johnson is an avid gun rights supporter and an influential member of the Tea Party faction. "I just knew she was looking to make a deal," I finished weakly.

"How?" Reines demanded.

"How?" I said.

Reines looked at Mills and Marshall, like *Holy shit can he really be this stupid?* "Who told you?"

I managed to hold my tongue long enough to shake my head and realize he didn't know I had directly overheard the conversation. "I don't, I can't say...I'm not sure..."

"You fucking prick." Reines looked like he wanted to pop me. "Who did you tell?"

"No one." Finally the chance to tell the truth! "I didn't tell anyone."

"It's all over the Hill!" Reines fairly screamed. "We're *this* close to a floor vote and a done deal on the nominations, and suddenly the Republicans and the press are treating this like Iran-Contra! Every fucking senator is running the other way, scared to fucking death of getting this shit on them! The nominations are fucked!"

Mills stared at me throughout, waiting for Reines to finish and turn away from me in disgust. "Do you realize you're probably going to be subpoenaed?"

My heart was pounding. "No, I don't..."

Mills laid her hand on my wrist. "Tell us who told you. Let's trace this back to the source. We'll do the best we can to make your testimony irrelevant."

I truly hadn't said a word, not even to Bel, who had flipped out when the Klobuchar nomination was officially announced. I had had no intention of being that messenger.

Which meant the leak had come from someone else. My guess was Podesta, trying to score political points with the Bernie backers.

This realization gave me strength. "I didn't leak a damn thing."

"Bullshit," said Reines.

Looking at the 3 of them, Hillary's closest aides, I think I saw a great deal of stress. Congress was blocking the administration's ability to spend more than symbolic funds on the jobs stimulus. And for all the bills introduced in Congress representing Hillary's pet projects and campaign promises, none had been reconciled between the 2 chambers.

The administration's major accomplishments consisted of reversing Trump's edicts and adding rules to existing laws, most of which were being vociferously challenged in Congress and the courts. The administration was hungry for a win, and now the Supreme Court vacancies—the real plums—were going to remain unfilled and leave the Clinton team starving.

"I knew Hillary was trying to swing a deal to get Klobuchar confirmed, but I didn't know who she was dealing with. Grassley and Johnson? News to me."

Mills looked sorry for me. "You've never been in front of a congressional investigation panel with the television cameras running, have you? I'm sad to say, for most people it's the kiss of death for your career. Politics or otherwise."

I smelled a bluff. Political deals were struck all the time, and never by the light of day. "My time in the hot seat will be short, at least. I really have nothing to tell."

They stared at me for some time. Then they gazed at each other. Then they asked me to leave.

As I passed through Reines' outer office, one of his admins was telling Hillary's nervous media relations specialist to have a seat. The media lady seemed to understand she wasn't there for an induction ceremony into Hillary's inner circle.

I hadn't been singled out for suspicion, it turned out. Reines, Mills and company were on a witch hunt, and I had come away floating (if I remember correctly, witches in New England always sunk), deemed innocent.

The next day, my security badge still worked.

PRESSER

O N OCTOBER 12TH, HILLARY SUCCUMBED to what had become a bipartisan outcry and held a press conference. She came to the podium joking about her warm relationship with the media. But it didn't take long for her distaste to show for the unscripted format.

An *Associated Press* reporter started in. "Mrs. President, you've issued by our count 42 regulations that most agree are 'powers of the purse' that is in fact constitutionally reserved for Congress. How do you respond?"

Hillary laughed. "Well as you know, for many years now Congress has abdicated that responsibility. 'Presided over their own obsolescence,' I believe is a quote I heard recently. The country simply can't function without a functioning government. From education to healthcare to immigration, we need leadership, and in many cases we urgently need action. We've had no choice but to step into the breach created by Congress."

A *Wall Street Journal* reporter followed on that. "But there's no constitutional authority for the president to step into that breach."

"I would say there is," said Hillary. "We are faithfully executing the law of the land, which if I'm not mistaken includes a functioning society."

"I'm sure some would argue that," said the *WSJ* reporter, "but that's not my question. You've increased federal spending and involvement to unprecedented levels, crippling private industry. Two examples are health insurance and banking. You've launched 2 new massive federal businesses, US Health and the Bank of the United States, which compete directly with the private sector. In doing so you've made it practically impossible for insurance companies and community banks to operate profitably. This in turn is leading to large-scale consolidation in these industries, so that only giant companies can survive. Is that your intent?"

"Well first of all, that might have set the record for a reporter's preamble," Hillary joked acidly. "How nice of your fellow reporters to give up some of their allotted time. But let me respond by saying, of course we're not promoting consolidation. Just the opposite. But if the health insurance and banking industries can't competitively price their services affordably for the American people, then I think we can all agree that change and real competition were long overdue. I'm frankly proud of what we've accomplished thus far."

She held up a finger while taking a drink of water. "Finally, I'll say we're looking into the appropriateness of the mergers."

"So even though it's the government squeezing out the small and mid-size companies and putting them in the position of dying or being acquired, you might disallow the mergers?"

"Like I said, we're looking into it."

"Mrs. President," said a *Los Angeles Times* reporter, "with the increased wages from the government stimulus has come a surge in border crossings. Has there been a conscious decision by your administration to look the other way?"

"I would say," said Hillary, "we as a nation haven't come to grips with the need for a comprehensive immigration solution. As you know, Congress has never appropriated funding for the wall begun by my predecessor."

"What about the stimulus money?"

"That's for infrastructure investments. I don't know too many people who consider a border wall to be infrastructure."

"A lot of people in the Southwest would consider it exactly that," said the *LA Times* reporter.

"Well I don't."

"There are reports," said a CBS television reporter, "that some of the stimulus jobs are being given to undocumented immigrants."

"No job is *given* to anyone, let me assure you," said Hillary. "They have to be earned. That being said, I'm not aware of any undocumented individuals being employed by the federal government."

"How about by companies receiving federal stimulus dollars?" the reporter pressed.

"I said I'm not aware. If you'd like, I'll have someone look into it."

"Switching gears," said a BBC correspondent, "to the war in the Middle East."

"To be accurate," said Hillary, "there is no war in the Middle East. At least not one in which the US is participating."

"Okay," said the correspondent. "How would you characterize the state of the US actions there?"

"Of course you'd have to ask Defense Secretary Flournoy to get a comprehensive answer. But I'd call it provisionally positive. We have a strong coalition of partners assisting us in bringing Iran's nuclear program to heel. Our bombing campaign is largely finished, and we believe we have eliminated or reduced Iran's nuclear capabilities significantly."

"How do you know?"

"We don't, not 100%. But if 100% was the standard, I don't know that you could call any military engagement in our history a success. We're extremely confident we've achieved what we set out to do. We're extremely proud of the damage we've inflicted on the Iranian regime at the cost of very few American lives. We treasure the lives of each and every one of our servicemen and servicewomen, and we do everything we can to avoid putting them in jeopardy unnecessarily."

"There are reports," said a *Bloomberg* reporter, "that Iran is ramping up its funding for al Qaeda and even ISIS-affiliated terrorist groups."

"They've been doing that for many years," said Hillary.

"Is that a problem?"

"Of course it is," Hillary snapped at the woman. "We have extensive efforts to counteract any Iranian funding. More importantly we're focusing our efforts on the root cause of the rise in worldwide terrorism. In Iran for instance we're already increasing our outreach efforts to the dissident community, and supporting various development initiatives. We are providing opportunities for the Iranian people and businesses that are currently denied by their government."

"The US is simultaneously providing funding while bombing Iran?"

"There's a theory called smart power. I pioneered it at the State department, incidentally. It stresses the importance of using carrots side by side with the sticks. Experience shows one doesn't work without the other. We're also imposing tough sanctions against military commerce, and encouraging our UN Security Council partners to join us."

"But they're not joining you, are they?" said the BBC correspondent.

"Yes, as a matter of fact your government, Great Britain, is joining us."

"But currently no one else, correct?"

"Like I said," said Hillary, "we're working with the Security Council to do just that."

A *Reuters* reporter was recognized. "Let's talk about Russia and Vladimir Putin."

"I'd rather not," Hillary joked.

The reporter waited out the very limited laughter. "Russia ostensibly has been working to create what is being referred to as a Shiite corridor, from Iran, through Iraq, to Syria and Lebanon. The Saudis, Jordanians, Turks and Egyptians are extremely concerned this is provoking a Sunni backlash and pushing the region closer to a sectarian war. Has the US traded one evil—an ISIS caliphate—for something worse?"

"We haven't *traded* anything for anything," said Hillary. "Alliances in the Middle East are constantly shifting. As you know, they can be tribal as much as sectarian. I think it's a constant challenge for the leaders over there to find an appropriate balance. As I said before, development and outreach continue to be necessary. And not just in Iran."

The *Reuters* reporter pressed forward. "Are you concerned that Russia is establishing a Cold War-style hegemony in the Middle East that might be antithetical to US and Western interests—as well as existentially dangerous for Israel?"

"Well as I already pointed out numerous times," said Hillary, "our best intelligence tells us we have incapacitated Iran's nuclear abilities. So we have *reduced* the existential threat to Israel."

"The Israeli prime minister doesn't seem to agree with that assessment," said the reporter. "He calls the current conditions the most unstable and dangerous for Israel in history."

"It's important to note," said Hillary sharply, "that *instability* doesn't equate to threats to Israel's *existence*. Again, we have reduced that threat. And never has US military strategy perfectly coincided with Israel's. We have different national interests."

A *Washington Post* reporter asked to be next to receive Hillary's ire. "Would you say the same for the nations of the Baltics? As you know—"

"I know exactly what my predecessor allowed in the countries of Lithuania, Latvia and Estonia," Hillary cut him off. "He basically created a *fait accompli*. We're now forced to accept the current situation, short of going to war with Russia."

"Is that on the table?"

"No it's not."

"Do you accept," the *Post* reporter pressed, "that once a NATO member has been invaded, the NATO treaty obligations are null and void?"

"That's a ridiculous question," Hillary raised her voice. "Our NATO obligations are alive and well, let me assure you. However, the conditions *as they stand* force us to take different approaches. One of those—one of *many*, I might add—is to reinforce the border with Poland and send a clear signal to Russia that enough is enough."

The *Post* reporter was intrepid. "Will we put troops in the Baltics, at the new borders created by the corridor Russia has effectively annexed?"

Hillary nodded for some time. "That's something we're exploring, one option among many."

"Could you expand on those options for us?"

"No, not at this time, no."

"How about Moldova and Romania?" another reporter called out from the crowd. "Do we plan to deploy US troops there as well?"

"At this very moment? No. But rest assured—and Secretary Petraeus and I have made this *very* clear to Mr. Putin and foreign minister Lavrov—nothing is off the table."

"Mrs. President, changing gears," said a *Politico* reporter. "Are you apprehensive at all about the recommendations due to be announced by the presidential election commission 3 days from now?"

Hillary simultaneously appeared to hear a voice behind her that none of us had registered. "Thank you, ladies and gentlemen. That's all we have time for today."

ELECTION R$_X$

O N OCTOBER 15TH, SPEC, THE 9-member Special Presidential Election Commission, released their prescription for changes to the system. They had an attractive young woman deliver the message.

"The One Person One Vote, or 1P1V movement as it has become known, had a big impact on our deliberations. And so, today we call on the various state legislatures to immediately move away from a win-ner-takes-all approach, to a process where electoral votes are awarded proportionate to their states' popular vote.

"This is a crucial change that will empower every voter to know that his or her vote does indeed count.

"We understand there are arguments for the current winner-takes-all system. But we believe the drawbacks of this approach far outweigh the limited benefits.

"Because a proportional system will increase the odds that no candidate reaches the required 270 electoral votes, we believe a second change needs to occur. The proportional system should be coupled with a ranking, instant run-off process. This companion process will also allow for meaningful participation by 3rd-party candidates.

"In the ranking, instant run-off system, every voter ranks his or her preferences on the ballot. For example, 1st choice is Candidate V, 2nd choice is Candidate Z, 3rd choice is Candidate X, and so on. If one candidate receives more than half of the 1st-choice votes, the election is over and electoral votes are awarded proportionately.

"If no candidate receives more than half of the 1st-choice votes, then the last-place candidate, say Candidate W, is eliminated, and ballots that had ranked Candidate W first are reassigned to those voters' 2nd choice.

"For instance, if you ranked Candidate W first and Candidate X second, and Candidate W is eliminated from the run-off, Candidate X would now receive your 1st choice. If one candidate now has more than 50% of the vote, say Candidate X with 55%, Z with 35% and V with 10%, the contest is over, and electoral votes are awarded proportionately. Otherwise the cycle is repeated.

"While this may sound complicated, in practice it is very straightforward. This approach is being utilized in a number of state and local elections. Under this ranking, instant run-off system, your vote for a 3rd-party candidate is never wasted. If your first choice doesn't make the run-off, your vote will still count, being cast for your next-favorite candidate.

"We are scheduling the presidential election for Tuesday, December 5th. We know this is a very short timeframe; but we also know that the country needs resolution sooner than later. And we think most Americans would agree, a compressed campaign season isn't a bad thing.

"By combining ranking, instant run-off with proportional electoral voting, we ensure every vote counts, and that one candidate is likely to win the minimum necessary number of electoral votes.

"In order to implement the new system before our next election, we urge the state legislatures to implement both of these systems immediately. We believe these changes are crucial to give the American people faith in their election process.

"We fervently hope and pray for a civil, competitive and ultimately rewarding 2017 presidential election. May God bless these United States of America."

POLITICS: NOT FOR
EVERYONE

THAT SAME DAY, DONALD TRUMP released a statement to the media.

"After careful consideration, I have decided not to run for president in the upcoming election. I have enjoyed serving this great country and thank everyone for their support. However, I believe my passion and energy and unique skills can be better employed in better fashion than as president. I wish the candidates all the success, and hope for a peaceful election. God bless America."

I had lunch the next day with Bel at a diner frequented by the political set. I say 'diner' but don't think fry grease in the air and a cig behind the waitress's ear. Their 'classic' burger was laced with braised veal and set me back $18.95. Different waiters take your order, refill your water and deliver your meal. Bel asked for a black (linen) napkin to match her skirt, and let her anguish fly.

"Why does our side always get screwed?!"

She was probably echoing half the restaurant; but without the practiced undertone.

Quietly I said, "I'm sure the other side says the same thing, half the time."

"Not in my lifetime," she lamented. "I was born too late. I didn't get to experience Reagan."

"It wasn't all wine and roses then either."

She shook her head at me. She looked ready to cry.

With Trump stepping aside, Hillary filed a petition that morning with the Supreme Court, asking them to certify the results of last year's election, allowing her to finish the remaining 3 years of the term. Constitutional scholars' handicapping odds were in her favor.

"Not that I'll miss this place," said Bel. "I never thought I'd be eager to get back to Detroit."

"Huh."

She read my frown as I chewed. "Don't tell me they've asked you to stay?"

"No. They haven't asked."

She dropped her salad fork. "Don't tell me you'd stay if they did?"

I bobbed my head.

"What? How could you? Aren't you sickened by every moment you're around them? This morning Hillary announced a new plan to boost the housing market—the one that she destroyed!"

"Refundable tax credits to offset the rising interest rates on mortgage loans," I described the plan.

"There isn't a government-caused problem that a government program can't fix," Bel railed. "How can you stand being around that?!"

I sipped my trendy D.C. drink, the Arnie Palmer Tribute—lemonade, tea and a sprig of edible grass—until people at the surrounding tables returned their attention to their meals. "I'm not you, honey."

"I know. I know. But still...." Her shoulders sagged in misery. "I don't want to be here, with her there. I don't know how you can take it."

"It's interesting as hell."

Bel stared at me. "You think they'd ask you? They don't even like you."

Hillary's team tolerated me. That was the best I could say. Nothing had changed after the Supreme Court nomination debacle—they trusted me no more and no less. I knew it was very possible that both the Imperfect Compromise and their tolerance would end simultaneously.

But yeah I enjoyed it. I think I was addicted to it, to tell you the truth. I wasn't sure anything else could ever compare to being inside the political machine.

"I would describe it this way," I told Bel. "Every discussion seems mean-ingful. Every meeting might include—"

Bel held up her hand. She was staring at the TV on the wall, along with most everyone in the diner.

Israel was being attacked.

"You're going to have to pick up the tab," I told Bel as I left the table. "Box the rest of my burger…"

IRAN, AGAIN

IN THE SITUATION ROOM HILLARY asked for an assessment. Defense Secretary Flournoy spoke.

"Early reports, it's not nuclear. Nothing dirty. The Israelis are getting hit by Hamas from the south, Palestinian Islamic Jihad from the east, Hezbollah from the north. Everything is coordinated, no doubt by Iran. It's a fair bet this is retaliation for our bombing campaign."

"Because we put the Iranians in a position where they have nothing left to lose," said Petraeus.

"They put themselves in that position," said Hillary.

"I'm talking strategically, not morally."

"How bad is the damage?" said Hillary.

"So far," said Flournoy, "18 Israelis dead and a couple hundred injured. That's going to pale in comparison to what Israel is going to do to them."

"And well they should," said Hillary. "That's the only negotiating language the other side understands."

"And that's why we failed by not forcing a regime change," said Petraeus.

Homeland Secretary Jake Sullivan jumped in. "That's the definition of *blind* power, not smart. We're not Israel. The Iranian people aren't going to hate us till the end of time. Not if we focus on the things they need to make better lives for their families. We don't dictate; we empower."

Petraeus seethed. "You couldn't be more wrong. Behind every implacable foe, you see the green, green grass of brotherhood. Hillary had it right: force is all the mullahs understand."

"The *mullahs!*" said Sullivan. "Yes! Not the *people.*"

"The people don't want a US-empowered future," said Petraeus. "You are dead wrong there. No, wait, the Israelis are dead. You're just wrong."

"Okay, okay," said Hillary. "We need to get past this. For the record, I agree with Jake—"

Petraeus slammed his briefing book on the table. "Then for the record, he needs to be your secretary of state."

"No, General," said Hillary. "We just need to talk through this."

"No, Mrs. President." Petraeus was on his way out. "It doesn't have to be what's-his-face. But you do need to name a new secretary. I resign." He closed the door behind him.

The room was quiet.

Hillary stared at the table. "Michèle," she said at length, "draw up a plan to support Israel. Whatever it takes. We treat this as bigger than a simple terrorist attack. If you think a counterattack on Iran is necessary, include that, too." She looked very tired as she followed Petraeus out the door.

I followed, too. Waiting for her in the anteroom was former president Obama. "Hillary," he said. "I know this is bad timing. But do you have a few minutes?"

"Barack, it's good to see you." Hillary dismissed me with a wave. "I always have time for you."

Together, just the 2 of them, they stepped into an adjacent office and closed the door.

THAT NIGHT I WAS TOLD by Cheryl Mills that absolutely nothing would be going down at the White House, and so I might as well go home. Hillary had retired to her quarters with Bill. I heard that Chelsea had arrived, too.

Still, I stayed late at my office in the basement of the West Wing to fulfill a part of my duties. Self-appointed duties, because they had never been defined, not by Trump who issued edicts and moved on, and not by Hillary who brought to the office her own already-established public-private initiatives to strengthen the black community, the Hispanic community, the LGBT community, etc. My self-appointed duties included a daily blog, a week-in-review e-letter, and an end-of-the-month talking points video blast.

Being who I am, I always started recording my end-of-the-month video on the 10th of the month, knowing full well it would change repeatedly and drastically over the next 3 weeks, but otherwise unable to sleep knowing it was unfinished.

As I left my basement office a little after 9 that night, I saw Hillary and Bill walking hand in hand down the hallway toward the kitchen. Hillary's eyes were red from crying. Bill's were redder.

The next morning the White House was abuzz with news of the US's destruction of Iranian oil distribution facilities in the Persian Gulf and multiple terrorist training camps supported by Iran, throughout the Middle East.

Bigger yet, the Israelis appeared to be expanding their borders, broadening the erstwhile Golan Heights into Lebanon and Syria, leapfrogging the West Bank into Jordan, and smashing through the Gaza Strip into Egypt. Practically every Arab group and nation was already calling it genocide and appealing to the UN.

Hillary was nowhere to be seen. Then just before 2 p.m. she went live from the Oval Office.

"The world today is convulsing from Iran's heinous, criminal attacks on Israel and the resulting warfare and bloodshed occurring as I speak. I want to make it clear that the US stands with Israel and its people in doing everything we can to protect them from harm.

"Israel has taken aggressive and offensive measures to do what they believe is necessary to protect their people and preserve their very existence. While we do support Israel, we will be reviewing these actions, and we warn all sides to respect the rules of war, the Geneva conventions, and to take all steps to protect innocent lives. There can be no excuse or absolution for any combatant to ignore the international standards of human rights established by law and worldwide consensus.

"I also have one other announcement to make. The timing is extremely unfortunate, but the timing could never be good, for me or my family.

"As you know, the Clinton legacy is one of service. And I will continue to serve the people of this nation and this world. The less fortunate, the sick and the poor. And especially the women who still struggle around the world and even here at home for basic human rights and dignity.

"I will no longer lead this struggle from the White House. I will not run for reelection for the remainder of this term. After extensive consultation with my family and a number of extremely close friends, whose opinions I value so, so deeply…"

Hillary choked up for a few moments before regaining composure.

"I believe it's in my best interests, and more importantly the interests of this country which I love, and for which I have devoted so much…"

Again she was temporarily overcome with emotion. "I will not put my name on the ballot next month. I am grateful for all the incredible effort put forth by the 9 members of the Presidential Election Commission, and for what I believe are significant, meaningful reforms to our electoral process.

"I urge the various state legislatures to adopt the recommendations. I believe it will lead to more accountability from our politicians, and more engagement from our citizens. I encourage our best and brightest from each party—from all parties—to step into this noble ring and compete for what I believe is the greatest job on earth.

"And so I will step down effective with the inauguration of our next president of these United States. Until then I promise you, I will continue to work night and day to ensure the prosperity and safety of every man, woman and child in this great country.

"Thank you again. And God bless America."

A day later Republican Marco Rubio and Democrat Kirsten Gillibrand were put forward by their respective parties to run for president. They held a debate that weekend. It was the first of 5 over the next month, and it included Libertarian Gary Johnson and the Green party's Jill Stein, who were each rapidly gaining support.

By the middle of November, 15 states had adopted proportional electoral voting, 9 states had adopted ranking, instant run-off voting, and another 8 states had adopted both. In the 18 states that adopted neither, emotional protests took place, right up to election day.

With no time or stomach for mail-in voting, every precinct in the nation required old-fashioned, day-of, in-person voting.

And on Tuesday December 5th, 2017 Americans went back to the polls....

Allan would like to thank our imperfect, beautiful nation for the limitless freedom to watch true characters attempt the wildly improbable, providing writers with such wonderful material.

Jason would like to thank Allan for writing stories about him.

Allan would like to thank Jason for staying alive long enough to write a few together.

Jason thanks God for all that and more.

ALSO BY HARRIS GRAY

Vampire Vic
Book 1 in the Vampire Vic Trilogy

Vampire Vic² Morbius Reborn
Book 2 in the Vampire Vic Trilogy

Vampire Vic III Sacrifice
Coming October 2016

★

Java Man

An Extra Shot from the Java Man

ABOUT THE AUTHORS

He's a Republican atheist, and he's a Christian who casts his vote for the candidate, not the party. Okay he's pretty much a Democrat. And they can't get enough of each other! They're a modern-day Matalin and Carville (assuming they're still together). They get it done at Crowfoot Valley Coffee and the Crowbar in Castle Rock, Colorado. They have lovely wives, crazy-good kids, and nice enough pets, some of which are edible.

The website: harrisgray.com
The marketplace: amazon.com/Harris-Gray
The tweets: twitter.com/harrisandgray
The posts: facebook.com/HarrisGrayAuthor
The sharing:
plus.google.com/u/3/102066651638902173967
The community: www.goodreads.com/harrisgray

www.ingramcontent.com/pod-product-compliance
Lightning Source LLC
Chambersburg PA
CBHW020619130626
46552CB00003B/1046